OLE'S PROMISE

by DORIS STENSLAND

Cover Drawing by Doris Stensland

Copyright © 1992 by
Doris Stensland

First Printing 1992

Library of Congress
Card Catalog No. 92-91038

ISBN 1-880552-02-7

Printed in United States of America

PINE HILL PRESS, INC.
Freeman, S. Dak. 57029

Dedication

To my grandchildren —
Kristen, Joseph, Sarah, Matthew,
Jeremy, Brian and Jonathan
four of whom live in the house that Ole built.

Preface

This fictional work is grounded in historical fact, and reveals a period in the life of Ole Christian Nordlie, my maternal grandfather.

I was twelve years old when my grandfather passed away, and at that time I did not know much about the early years of his life. My childhood memories are mainly of him being tired and overworked, but enjoying his cup of coffee and the necessary sugar lumps.

Twelve years ago we were informed of the existence of thirty-one letters my grandfather, Ole Nordlie, had written to his sister and brother-in-law in Norway, over a period of more than thirty years. Reading these letters has given me a better knowledge of his thoughts, feelings and the activities of these early years. In fact, they helped acquaint me with this man who was my grandfather.

I am grateful to the Rognlien family in Skreia, Norway, for the opportunity to see the letters, and also for many facts given by Odd Rognlien, my mother's cousin, who I am sorry to report, will not get to read this book because he passed away earlier this year.

A "thank you" to my mother who has shared with me many of the happenings of her youth, and of life in the first part of the 1900's, and who has been patiently waiting for the completion of this book.

My appreciation goes out to the Canton Public Library for their help, and for information gleaned from old *Sioux Valley News* and *Dakota Farmers Leader* newspapers.

There are two people who have given me special assistance, namely Gary Schultz and Ann Foland, who edited the book for me. I am very grateful to them both.

I also wish to thank my friends and family who encouraged me, especially my daughter Susan, who has helped me in many ways, and, most of all, my husband Hans for the contribution he made to it.

Ole Nordlie, age 22—Circa 1888.

Chapter I

At day's end, Norway's Hurdal valley lay in stillness. The birds' evening songs, which earlier had been re-echoed by the surrounding mountains, now were hushed. An occasional light zephyr danced lazily across the land and in its path left a leaf trembling or a branch gently swaying.

A horse's whinny broke the silence. Coming down the narrow road was a primitive wagon, drawn by a team of horses. The empty wagon bounced along over the rough trail. Young Ole Christian Nordlien shook the reins lightly and encouraged his team with a "Geddap, *hesten* (horses), we'll soon be home."

It was May, 1887, and the Hurdal valley was coming alive after the long winter. Once more the landscape was beginning to be transformed into the vivid greens of a Norwegian summer.

Ole Christian Nordlien and his team and wagon were returning from their weekly trip to Dal Station for the Hurdal Glassverks. Because the railroad had not been routed into the Hurdal valley, the glass factory's lovely products were transported to Dal Station, the closest railroad stop, by horse and wagon. Ole Christian Nordlien was one of their freight haulers.

Now Ole Nordlien and his wagon left the valley as higher and higher the team pulled the wagon up the steep trail until it reached the upper slopes where the huge barn, *stabbur* and large house of the Nordlien farm were located. Ole Christian jumped down from the wagon and unhitched his team. This slim man of medium height was twenty-two years of age, with muscular shoulders and calloused hands. On his wide upper lip grew a light brown mustache, which he cultivated to present a look of maturity.

Ole Christian led his team into the barn and tossed them hay to eat while he unharnessed them. After hanging the harnesses on the pegs on the wall, he gave each horse a kind slap on its flank.

"Did you have a good trip?" a voice called from the barn doorway. It was Marte Nordlien, his mother. This woman of small stature and neat appearance, had an almost limitless energy as she daily moved from one task to another. But she wore a sad expression and she didn't smile much any more.

It had been almost a year now since the Nordlien farm had lost its owner — Lars Ulrickson Nordlien. After his sudden death, Marte, his widow, had taken charge of the *gaard* (farm). Now she was checking on her second oldest son, Ole Christian.

"The horses seem tired, Ole. Do you think those long trips to Dal Station are too hard on them?"

"When they get something to eat, they'll be all right," her son assured her.

Marte Nordlien gave a deep sigh, "The hauling contract with the Hurdal Glassverks has certainly been a help to us this past year."

Ole Christian took some papers from his pocket, "Here, Mother, is the payment for today's trip."

She accepted it and almost in a whisper confided, "You're a good son, Ole." She put the papers in her pocket and added, "But you should be using this for your own future."

Ole Christian knew how difficult it had been for his mother since his father's death. He had only admiration for the way she had managed *Nordlien.* Ole Christian and younger brother, Ludvig, and two younger sisters lived in the big house with their mother. Older brother, Laurits, and his wife and young son, resided in an adjacent cottage. All contributed to the on-going of *Nordlien.*

This evening Ole had a good feeling. Summer was at hand in Hurdal and the excitement of a new season of growth was running in his veins. The family had pulled together and come through the past year of difficulties and grief. Now that all lay behind them. It was spring and he looked ahead with hope to the future.

Mother and son walked side by side to the house. It wasn't only the horses that were hungry. Ole Christian had had a long day with only a small lunch and now he looked forward to a bowl of hot porridge . . . and with it, a cold glass of buttermilk.

Vaar (Spring) was the busy time of the year. The patches of rye and wheat had to be sown, and potatoes planted. When the grass was growing on the *seter,* the cows and sheep were moved up to Snultra to the high pastures. Besides the other tasks, the two trips to Dal Station had to be made each week—on Fridays by Ole Christian and on Tuesdays by his older brother, Laurits.

Before long, the hay was tall enough to cut. On a pleasant July forenoon the men and women from the three tenant cottages, together with Marte Nordlien's own family, assembled to help with the haying.

Marte paused and leaned on her rake as she inspected the haying operation. She watched the men wielding their scythes, with son, Ole Christian, in the lead. Marte felt pride in this son. He swung his scythe with a regular rhythm—not wasting any motions. He was the one who had inherited her father's agricultural talents. Working with the land and the animals came naturally for him. A born farmer. Yet, it saddened her to realize that though he may have inherited farming talents, he never would inherit farm land on which to practice them . . . for this son was the second-born.

Marte bent over her rake, arranging a pile of hay for the men to load in the cart her oldest son, Laurits, was driving. As she worked, she planned ahead. Her mind was on Gunda, the milkmaid, who was up at the *seter* caring for the Nordlien cows and sheep. She must send Ole Christian up to the summer pastures on Sunday for it had been several weeks since anyone had been to Snultra to check on Gunda and the animals.

Marte's back began to tire. She slowly straightened and looked around at this pleasing scene of men and women bending over their scythes and rakes and the horse chewing on stalks of hay as it waited while the cart was being loaded.

Ja, work was good for both people and animals. It kept them in shape. Yes, and work had another reward. It gave the feeling of accomplishment. When this hay was piled high in the barn, yes, that would be her reward. And it was good to keep busy, for then she didn't think of her grief or her loneliness for Lars.

4

Chapter II

"**C**ome now, Mathilda," Marte Nordlien called to her ten-year-old daughter. "Don't dawdle. *Prest* Leganger won't wait services for us."

After a stern *"Skynde seg"* (Hurry up!), her daughter came running, carrying one shoe in each hand.

"Do I have to wear my shoes, Mother?" she begged. The summer months were barefoot time for Mathilda, and shoes felt so confining.

"Such foolishness, Mathilda! Of course, you do. Why, we are going to God's house."

Marte instructed her daughter to sit down and put on her shoes.

Marte's older daughter, Ingeborg, stood inside the door waiting for them. Finally, she put her *skaut* (kerchief) over her brown hair. Today the braids were arranged in a coil by each ear. Short whisps of hair hung loosely around her face and peeked out of the kerchief. Ingeborg was a beautiful young girl of eighteen, slender and petite. She was the one her mother depended on to help with the housework and get the meals and lunches for the family and the workers. She picked up the bunch of flowers her mother had gathered, which would be placed on her father's grave today.

"NOW we must hurry!" Marte urged as she took Mathilda by the hand and headed for the door.

As she opened it, she turned and called, "Ole Christian, the sack with provisions for Gunda is here by the door. Don't forget it!"

With that, Marte and her two daughters disappeared down the trail towards the white Hurdal church, which was located way down in the valley beside the Hurdal Lake.

Ole Christian picked up the sack and slung it over his shoulder, then headed upwards from the farm buildings towards Snultra, the *Nordlien seter.*

It was a beautiful Sunday morning as he took the path that led to the top of the small mountain behind his home. His little sister, Mathilda, had mentioned the strawberries were ripe so he went a little out of his way to check on the wild strawberry patch that lay on the edge of the woods. Yes, the little berries were red. He picked a handful. They were so sweet he bent to pick more, then started on his way again, lunching on berries.

Ole walked alongside the creek where the lily of the valley had been blooming several weeks earlier. Following along the edge of the woods that almost covered this section of *Nordlien*, Ole made a note to himself to come up soon and mark the trees to be harvested this fall. The birch trees were beautiful now with their white bark and green leaves, and the fir trees of all sizes stretched up towards the skies.

The sound of church bells made him stop and listen. From the Hurdal church in the valley, the tones of the bells echoed and re-echoed as the sounds bounced from one mountain across to the other. *Yah, that was music!*

Ole surveyed the world from this high position. Across the valley was another mountain. Around him and above him were the *Nordlien* forests. Nestled here and there at different levels on the mountains were many little farms. This was his world.

Ole continued his upward climb. Before he reached Snultra the cowbells could be heard, first faintly, and then clearer as he came nearer the little cabin where he would deliver the provisions. The door stood open.

"Gunda," he called.

"Oh, it's you, Ole. Just a minute and I'll be with you."

Gunda was busy filling the wooden vats with the morning's milk. Earlier the cream had been skimmed from yesterday's milk and the wooden pans washed. She was concentrating on her work.

Gunda was a short and chunky woman of about fifty years, whose lifelong work had been managing the cows at *Nordlien*. She loved the animals, and relished the rich cream and butter they produced.

Ole set down his sack and stood by the door while Gunda finished her milk chores. Here he could look out and see the cows and sheep, contented and grazing on the lush green grass of the *seter*. Seated on a rock near them was Kjersti, the twelve year old daughter of one of the tenant families. This year it was she who had come as Gunda's helper. Kjersti knitted as she kept watch of the livestock.

When Gunda finished, she wiped her hands on her apron and came to inspect what Ole had brought.

"Yah, we have been waiting for someone from *Nordlien*. We were getting low on flour, and we haven't had sugar for several days." She set the flour and sugar on the table.

Now Gunda's business-like attitude changed to one of sociability as she invited, "*Sette seg* (sit down), Ole. You must have something to eat before you start back."

From the corner table she picked up a small wooden pan of *rommebunke* (soured milk). At this time of year the temperature was just right to set the milk in a solid mass, leaving a top layer of cream, and the combination was neither sour nor bitter.

Gunda set it down before Ole as she teased, "See, I remember what you like." She then went to the fireplace where the coffee pot hung, and grabbing the hot handle with the bottom of her apron, she poured two cups of coffee and sat down at the table with Ole. After several swallows of the hot coffee, she wiped the perspiration from her forehead.

"Now, Ole," she instructed in her coarse voice, "be sure to tell your mother that Svaarteku had a fine heifer calf. That will mean another milk cow in several years."

Gunda took another drink of coffee. "And tell her that each cow fills one of the wooden pails. This fresh green grass is just what it takes to make milk."

Ole was enjoying the soured milk. With his spoon he was cutting a path around the edges of the *rommebunke*.

Gunda watched him. "Now, tell me what is happening at *Nordlien*."

Ole took another spoonful of the firm mixture.

"Well, we finished with the haying yesterday. It is now hanging on the '*hesje*' (racks) to dry."

Ole took a few sips of the coffee.

"Tell me, how are your mother and the girls? and Laurits and Karine and the little one?"

"Everyone is well. We have all been busy."

"Yah, I have been busy too. You'll have a big wooden pail of butter to take back with you . . . and some fine white cheese too." The tone of her voice revealed her pride in her accomplishments.

"*Well, what about you then, Ole? I've been wondering and wondering what you are going to do.*"

Ole was absorbed with his eating and didn't quite understand her question.

Gunda continued, "I figured by now you would be making plans to move out. It's been over a year since your father's death."

This statement caught Ole's attention and he raised his head and studied her. Gunda cleared her throat and explained, "Has everyone forgotten that Laurits has the *odelsret* (birthright)? He is the oldest, you know. Karine told me herself that Laurits and she would like to be in charge at *Nordlien* now that your father is gone."

Ole could hardly believe what he was hearing.

Gunda's voice trailed on, "Your mother will not turn the farm over to them as long as you are there to help. Of that I am sure!"

This topic took Ole by surprise. Ole had made no plans because he felt his mother needed him. Why, she would have to support ten-year-old Mathilda for a number of years yet. And furthermore, he did not intend to discuss family matters with Gunda.

Gunda took another drink of coffee to calm herself. She set her left elbow on the table and rested her chin on her hand as she thought about the situation that had gotten her so worked up. Suddenly she smiled and then chuckled to herself.

"The other day I was thinking about Laurits and that night . . . was it four or five years ago now? . . . when he and his friend came up here to Snultra late one night with the idea of visiting Kari, my helper that summer."

Gunda paused and chuckled some more. "Oh, that Laurits! He is the jolly one! Yah, Ole, I suppose you have heard this story plenty of times." She loved to tell this episode, which was one of the most exciting experiences of her routine life.

"Well, we were asleep and didn't hear the rap on the door, so those two rascals climbed up on the cabin roof, and Laurits' friend was going to slide down the chimney."

Now Gunda laughed out loud. "It was good enough for him! He was lowering himself, holding on the chimney edge and trying to get a toe-hold."

Here she used her hands and foot to make the story more vivid. "He was trying to get some footing when Laurits shot his gun into the air. The unexpected shot scared him and he let go. *Plup!* We were awakened by the shot and the landing of Carl in the fireplace."

She chuckled some more. "I'll never forget that night! Yah, that Laurits, he is the jolly one!"

Gunda gave Ole a sly sideward glance and added, "Now you, Ole, are the serious, hard-working one."

Gunda was getting the coffee pot again.

"*Nei, takk*! (No, thanks)" Ole told her. He left the last spoonfuls of *rommebunke* in the dish. Suddenly the soured milk didn't taste good. He got up from his chair and asked Gunda for the butter and cheese, for he was starting home.

These past months Ole had felt that life at *Nordlien* was becoming arranged again. Apparently that was not so. It bothered him that Laurits' wife had discussed things with Gunda. This whole subject was upsetting.

Ole picked up the wooden pails of butter and cheese and headed down the mountain, but he had something disturbing to think about as he made his homeward journey.

Friday was Ole Christian's day to drive to Dal Station. He climbed out of bed early so he would have ample time to feed and curry his team before he harnessed them.

Ole Christian had the horses out of the barn and was hitching them to the wagon when brother Laurits appeared.

"I'll be driving today," Laurits announced. He reached for the reins as he instructed, "Ole, you help Mother and Ludvig with the potato harvest today."

Ole wanted an explanation. "Did Mother tell you to change days?" he questioned.

"It doesn't matter. I'm driving today."

Ole Christian became upset. It was his mother who was managing the farm, and he didn't appreciate being ordered around by his brother. *Hadn't he gotten the horses ready?* . . . Besides, he had ordered a pair of shoes from a shoemaker at Dal, and he planned to pick them up that day. This was the weekend of the young people's *Høstfest,* and he intended to wear the new shoes Saturday night.

Laurits was persistent and proceeded to climb up on the wagon. Ole's anger accelerated. *He would stand up for his rights!* He would not have Laurits changing his plans.

Anger flushed through his whole body as he grabbed his brother's jacket and pulled him from the wagon. They scuffled and rolled on the ground, each trying to get the advantage over the other. Finally Ole gave his brother a good jab in his stomach. He didn't wait around but quickly climbed up on the wagon and drove off to the glass factory to pick up his load.

Ole Christian had all day to think about the situation. As he rode the miles to and from the Dal Station, he reviewed all the aspects of the situation. Of course, he knew that someday Laurits would inherit *Nordlien*. Laurits was the oldest, and he had the *odelsret*. That's the way it was. But this wasn't supposed to happen so soon. Mother was still too young to retire. Laurits was trying to rush things. Was Laurits only thinking of himself? . . . or did he consider what was best for their mother? and their sisters? Ole wondered.

The next morning Ole Christian went about his duties. When he came into the house for morning coffee, his brother Laurits was also there. Marte Nordlien poured coffee for her two sons, and passed a plate with slices of bread and cheese. The tension and ill feeling could be felt in the room. No one had anything to say as they ate their lunch.

Marte interrupted the silence. "I heard about your disagreement yesterday." The sad manner in which she said it showed it distressed her.

"Oh, my boys! Now that your father is gone, don't you know we must work together?"

She slowly turned her head from one son to the other.

"Oh, my boys! Why can't you two get along? Will you be like Jacob and Esau, always quarreling over each other's rights?"

It hurt Ole to see his mother unhappy. But something was changing. Ole Christian Nordlien was beginning to see that there wasn't room for both Laurits and him at Nordlien. And Laurits had the *odelsret*. However, as yet, he hadn't figured out what he was going to do about it.

Chapter III

Late Saturday afternoon the young people from *Nordlien* — Ole Christian, Ludvig and Ingeborg — headed down the mountain to the young people's *Høstfest*. As they came nearer the valley, they were met by the sounds of fiddles tuning up, and lots of laughter. Young men and women were gathering in groups. There was much excitement. Some of the girls had spent all summer up on the *seters*, and now they were happy to be with their friends again.

"Just let me know when you want to go home, Ingeborg," Ole Christian told his sister. "It is best if we don't stay too late. Mother will be listening for us."

Ingeborg hurried off to a group of her friends, and Ludvig disappeared among a crowd of young people. Ole stood and looked around. Then someone called his name.

"Ole, come over here." It was his cousin Isaac Hoel Lisbakken. Ole joined him.

"How's it going at *Nordlien*?" Isaac asked. "Did you get your potatoes out?"

"Yes, sir, and we got three sacks more than last year. How about you, Isaac?"

"No, we haven't finished. That way we'll have something to do next week. Right?" Isaac laughed.

"Say, Isaac, how is it you are sitting here alone?" Ole had caught a glimpse of Kari, Isaac's girl friend, as he walked through the groups of young people.

"Oh, that's another story, Ole. Things change. Now Kari has other interests. It seems a fellow from Hadeland has been visiting her all summer up at the *seter* . . . and now she is engaged to marry him."

Ole had a feeling of sympathy for his cousin.

"That's too bad, Isaac. I know you've had your eye on her for a long time."

"Oh, don't feel sorry for me. I have my mind on something bigger now" . . . and he emphatically added, *"and it isn't that girl!"*

Isaac took a letter from his back pocket.

"Here, Ole, I want you to read the letter I got from my old neighbor, Petter. It is over a year now since he went to America."

"I have been wondering how he was getting along."

Isaac handed the letter to Ole, who pulled it from the envelope and unfolded it.

> Wisconsin
> *Nord* America

Kjaere Isaac,

How are things back there in the Old Country? I often think of you and my other friends back there. Isaac, I tell you this is the life, living here in America. Yah, that was the best decision I've made so far in my 23 years.

I have a good hired man job here in Wisconsin. The man I work for is Norwegian and he immigrated twenty years ago. The best part is that he has three daughters, and they are all so beautiful I haven't decided yet which one is the best. I tell you, Isaac, they know how to grow pretty girls over here in America.

Say, Isaac, I can find you a job in this community if you want to come. It would be good to have my old friend here — and there are plenty of pretty girls to go around. Think about it and let me know.

> Your old pal,
> Petter

When Ole finished reading the letter, Isaac spoke. He was very serious. "I haven't told anyone yet, but I've decided to go to America."

Ole gave him a surprised look. "Isaac, is this all because Kari is engaged?"

"No, Ole, that has nothing to do with it. I have been thinking about it for some time. I've decided there isn't much future for me here in Hurdal. I have to step out, and from what I hear, America has many opportunities. Living in America is not so different. There are Norwegian communities there. *It isn't like going to Africa!*"

"Going to America is a big step, Isaac. When it comes right down to it, I wonder if you could really leave Norway and Hurdal."

The music had begun, and the young people were joining in folk dances. Round and round, they were weaving in and out of their circles, and bowing and dancing. The fiddles led the event with their loud, whining tones and rhythmic melodies.

Ole and Isaac continued with their conversation. Ole had something to share also. "I guess I'll be moving out next year too. I have to serve my year in the military and I may just as well get it over."

"I haven't served yet either, but if I go to America, I won't need to worry about that."

"Ole and Isaac," brother Ludvig called. "What are you two doing over there by yourselves? The girls are asking for you."

"Yah, I suppose we'd better be sociable," Isaac said. He put the letter back in his pocket and the two wandered over to where the music was playing, but Ole's shoes were new and stiff and he intended to spend most of the time watching and visiting.

Ole Christian and younger brother, Ludvig, trudged through the snow, leading their horse, Blakken. It was December and they had spent the past two weeks at the cabin where they had been felling trees on the upper slopes. The *Nordlien* forests held much good lumber, but it was hard work getting it harvested. Now they were on their way home. Their faithful horse, Blakken, had been needed to pull the fallen trees so they could be stacked, ready to be transported down to the valley in the spring.

Their mother met them at the door. They both were tired and hungry and it was good to get into a warm room again.

Marte quickly made a hot meal for them. She had begun her Christmas baking, and they were treated to some of the cookies and lefse she had been making.

Marte Nordlien brought the mail that had arrived while they were gone.

"We received a Christmas letter from *Tante* (Aunt) Berte in America this year," she said, and read it aloud for them.

Dear sister Marte and family,
   God Jul! (Merry Christmas)
   We have been settled here in Dakota Territory for two years already. We live near the Lars Sogns. You know, he married Mari Knain who lived there in Hurdal. This is a farming community, and I am talking about BIG farms. Most of them are 160 acres or more, compared to Norway's 10-20 acre patches. The fields here are large with hardly any trees, and the ground is level so it is much easier to work than the mountainous fields of Hurdal.

All our neighbors are Norwegian. Ole Hagbart says to tell Ole Christian and Ludvig that he knows of several hired men jobs if they are interested. Seriously, if they are interested, we will help them get settled here in Dakota Territory.

Have a good Christmas season and greet all our relatives when you see them.

Greetings,
sister Berte Grue
and family

The last two months Ole had been doing a lot of thinking. As he listened to *Tante* Berte's letter, something clicked. Yah, maybe that was the way he should go — join cousins Ole Hagbart and Kristian in America. Farming was the only thing he wanted to do and he would have little chance for that here in Hurdal, or in Norway, for that matter. He had been considering all the possibilities, and there weren't many from which to choose.

Ole needed to talk to someone. Tomorrow was Sunday. In the afternoon he would walk over to Lisbakken and have a visit with cousin Isaac. He wanted to find out how Isaac's America plans were coming. Yah, perhaps he could go along when Isaac went to America. Then he could forget about military duty also. Yes, he had to talk to Isaac. He would go see him tomorrow.

After Christmas, Ole Christian Nordlien began to make plans. Isaac was leaving from Christiania the last of April. Ole had decided to go also. He would need money for his ticket and some extra cash to live on until he got employment. He had finally told his mother of his decision and she had begun to cry. Ole had known it would be hard for her, yet he felt she really understood he had no future here in Hurdal.

Ole explained to his mother that he would be willing to put in many extra days and weeks harvesting the *Nordlien* forests if he could have some of the money when the lumber was sold in the spring. Ludvig and he would go again up to the cabin to cut the trees on the higher slopes.

Ole Christian was becoming excited about his America plans now. It helped that on weekends he and Isaac could talk together. But he really dreaded to see spring come because then he would have to say farewell to both his family and his land. *And at times he wondered if he could really say goodbye to Hurdal and Norway.*

April arrived, and with it the melting of the ice and snow which made the river begin to flow again so lumber could be floated down to the valley where it was sold to the lumber mill.

Ole hired a neighbor to build a large wooden chest and had his name and the year painted on the front of it. He was filling it with his belongings, which included the many pairs of socks and mittens his mother was knitting for him. She had heard stories of the fierce winters that came to Dakota and felt he needed a good supply.

The last few days before Ole left, his mother was very quiet, and often on the verge of tears. She felt she should give her son advice. *"Be a good Christian man, Ole. Yes, and always be honest. And don't be afraid of work.* You won't have trouble keeping a job if you remember those things."

Laurits was to drive Isaac and Ole Christian to the Dal Station where they would board the train for Christiania, and there get on the ship leaving for America.

During the last few weeks before his departure, there were times Ole had wished he could hold time back. It was passing so quickly. The day arrived and it was time to say goodbye. There was excitement, but not happiness, for hearts at *Nordlien* were heavy as Ole went from one loved one to the other.

Awkwardly he embraced his Mother. He had never been one to show his emotions. "Please don't cry, *Mor*," he pleaded. "It isn't like we won't see each other again. I'll be back in a few years to visit you. I promise, Mother."

Marte took his hand and held it, stroking it. Then she turned her back to him as she used her apron to wipe her eyes.

Ole put his arms around his two sisters, Ingeborg and Mathilda. "You girls look after Mother. When I come again, I'll take you two along back to America with me. I promise."

Ole shook his younger brother Ludvig's hand. "Take it easy, Ludvig. Will you join me in America if I find you a job?" Ole gave Ludvig's hand another shake and added, "You and Laurits take good care of Mother and the girls."

Ole's sisters were wiping their eyes.

Marte was reluctant to say the final *"Farvel."* As Ole bent down, she took his face in her two hands and lovingly patted his cheek, all the while staring at him as if she was memorizing each detail of his features. Then she turned and wiped her eyes again.

Ole climbed up on the wagon which already held his trunk and food supplies. He would take one last look at what had been his home these 23 years. His gaze extended across to the opposite mountain and to the scenes he had viewed all these years—the trees and the farms nestled here and there on the Hurdal slopes.

"We'd better go," Laurits reminded Ole. "Isaac will be waiting." This time of leaving had been just as painful as he had imagined it would be. He had a lump in his throat, and he bit his lip to hold back the tears. As they drove off, Ole turned and waved. He would always remember his dear ones standing there—Mother, wiping her eyes with her apron; Ingeborg and Mathilda, waving; and Ludvig, with his hand raised in the air.

Now Laurits and Ole began the downward journey from *Nordlien* to Lisbakken, and really, it was the beginning of his journey to America. Ole felt a little uncertain. He wondered what the future held for him.

Chapter IV

"Next stop . . . E-D-E-N," the conductor called out as he moved down the train aisle. Through the windows passed a panorama of farm countryside, with long stretches of treeless scenery. The lively *"chug-chug"* of the locomotive gradually began to slacken.

People who would be disembarking began collecting their belongings. The mother of the two little girls who had been running up and down the aisle set them down while she proceeded to put their bonnets and coats on them.

A young man seated towards the back of the passenger car, Ole Christian Nordlie by name, tightened his grip on the covered box he held in his lap. His thin brown hair was neatly parted and combed to each side. In his lap was a wooden box containing two slices of dry bread and several slivers of cheese. He and his cousin, Isaac Hoel Lisbakken, had purchased additional food in New York when they had arrived there from Norway six days ago, on May 10, 1888. After going through the Castle Gardens immigration halls, their next stop was Chicago. At the Castle Gardens, his name had in a mix-up of language and confusion been changed from Nordlien to Nordlie.

In Chicago these two Hurdal boys parted ways. Ole had boarded the train for Sioux City, Iowa, which was now taking him into Dakota Territory.

Ole picked up his hat. He wanted to be ready when the train stopped in Eden. His black coat and trousers were rumpled and soiled from living in them for over three weeks. Once more he glanced out the window and studied this land which was to be his hope for the future. He strained his vision to the farthest distance in search of a mountain. Surely the horizon would reveal mountains. But he could find none.

Eden, Dakota Territory, United States of America was a long way from Hurdal, Norway, where Ole Christian Nordlie had spent the first twenty-three years of his life. It pained him to think about *Nordlien,* his home, situated high on Nordli Kampen mountain in Norway. Deep down already he was homesick, but he had made his plans and he was determined to follow through. But there was a touch of bitterness in his heart. He felt like a bird that had been pushed from its nest.

The train whistle blew as it approached Eden, and the train finally came to a screeching stop. The people who were leaving arose and filed into the aisle. Ole remained seated. To be jostled around in all this commotion would only make him more confused. All he had been hearing lately was the American language, and it was foreign to him. He missed his cousin with whom he could *"snakke norsk"* (speak Norwegian).

Somewhere, a distance from Eden, lived Ole Christian Nordlie's Aunt Berte Grue and family. But how would Ole Nordlie be able to find them in this strange flat land where everyone spoke this language he could not understand? Finally he too arose, and followed the others out of the train.

In the depot many people were milling about. Passing near several men, Ole caught the sound of a Norwegian conversation. He moved closer and finally summoned enough courage to interrupt them. *"Unskyld?"* (Excuse me) he said.

"Yah? Is it something you want?" the older man asked in Norwegian.

Ole tried to explain his predicament to them. "I have just come from Norway and I want to go to my aunt's home west of this town. Could you tell me the way?"

The two men looked at Ole, and then they looked at each other and nodded their heads. The younger spoke, "Yah sure, we guessed you were a newcomer." He paused as he took a puff of his cigar.

"But tell me, who is it that you are looking for? I am a storekeeper here in town and I know alot of people around here."

Ole suddenly felt out of place. He was grimy from his travels, and he knew his suit was wrinkled. If only he had had a chance to scrub and put on clean clothes after his ocean voyage.

Finally he responded. "Grues . . . *Fru* Andreas Grue, and my cousins Ole Hagbart and Kristian."

"Gru-eh?" The man thought a moment and then answered, "There are some Gru-ehs living about seven or eight miles west of town. Yah, I know the boys. The mother doesn't come to town very often. They must be the ones you are looking for."

He took another puff of his cigar and slowly blew out the smoke.

"*Jamen, gutt* (boy)," he continued, "I think you are in luck. I saw a neighbor of theirs in town this afternoon. He had his lumber wagon and I would wager that you could get a ride out there with him."

He looked in the direction of the luggage platform, and added, "I'll help you find him, but first I must pick up a package that was to come on this train."

Ole breathed a sigh of relief. Things were working out. Soon he would be with family again. Suddenly a fearful thought came to him. He had to find out. "*Do these neighbors speak Norwegian*?" he asked.

"You bet!" the man answered. "That community west of Eden is all Norwegian. You won't need to learn to speak English there." He threw his cigar butt in the cuspidor and turned again to Ole, "Why don't we go and check on your trunk? They may have room to haul that also."

Ole's first days in Dakota Territory were very enlightening. So many things were different from Norway. How glad he was that he had his aunt and cousins to explain and teach him the ways of the New World.

Ole felt so much better after he had a chance to scrub himself and put on some of his cousins' clean clothes. Aunt Berte had taken all of his belongings, washed some things and hung others outside to air. "We have to get that ship smell out of them," she explained.

Ole's Aunt Berte and family lived on a rented farm in the heart of Norway Township, Lincoln County, Dakota Territory, about fifty miles north of Sioux City, Iowa. Berthe Grue had five boys, two of them older than Ole; the rest much younger. Aunt Berte was a sister of Ole's mother, Marte Nordlien, of Hurdal. The two older boys had immigrated to America in 1881, and their parents and the rest of the family had come later. Berte's husband, Andreas Grue, had died after arriving in the New Country. They had come to this community because Lars and Maria Sogn had homesteaded here. Berte and Maria were distantly related, and both came from Hurdal.

Several days after Ole's arrival, Ole and his two older cousins sat at the table and drank their forenoon coffee. Auntie Berte had cooked up some raw sugar, so there were sugar lumps also. She had piled these "*sukkerbits*" (sugar lumps) in a little crystal dish that immediately caught Ole's eye. The crystal dish reminded him of home.

"From the Hurdal glass factory?" he asked.

"Yes," replied Auntie Berte. "I brought several pieces along to America."

Berte filled their cups with more hot coffee. Ole poured a little in his saucer to cool.

Aunt Berte pulled the churn, which she had filled with cream, over by her chair and began the slow task of making butter while continuing with the conversation.

"Tell us about everyone in Hurdal," Aunt Berte begged. "How is your Mother? and Laurits and his family? And what is Ludvig doing now? and Ingeborg and Mathilda? I suppose they have changed a lot since we left."

Ole went down the list and brought her up to date on all of his family: Laurits, Ole's oldest brother, was married and had a son; brother Ludvig was two years younger than Ole; sister Ingeborg was a lady of nineteen and Mathilda was now eleven.

"Things are different at Nordlien since Pa died," Ole pointed out. "Mother has tried her best to manage the *gaard*, but she misses Pa very much."

The sun was shining through the east window and sunbeams were dancing on the table. The day was beginning to get warmer.

"The first thing you should do," said cousin Kristian, "is get yourself some different clothes. We don't wear wool here in America in the summertime. In a month or two you will feel a heat you never dreamed existed."

Ole already had noticed the warmer temperature and had rolled up his shirt sleeves. Already it was as warm as it ever got in Hurdal.

Aunt Berte broke in, "If you still have some money, Ole, you should go along to Eden with the boys. There are denim trousers that you can buy in town and cooler shirts. These clothes are easier to launder too."

Ole agreed, "Yah, when I go to work for that neighbor I need some practical clothes."

"You were mighty fortunate to pick up a job so soon," spoke up cousin Ole Hagbart.

"Yes," said Ole, "the neighbor who brought me out here asked if I had a job. When I told him I hadn't looked for one yet, he said he could use another hired man. He wants me to start next week."

"Those Thormodsgaards have some fine horses," announced his cousin.

Ole was glad to hear that. "I have had experience with horses. That kind of work I can do."

Ole sipped from his saucer and then brushed the edges of his mustache dry with the back of his hand. He reached for a sugar lump, dipped it into his coffee cup and deposited it in his mouth.

"Ole," Kristian advised, "don't be afraid to ask questions. Many things are done differently here in America."

He cleared his throat and explained, "First you'll have to cultivate corn. This you know nothing about.

"Then," he continued, "you'll have to help with the haying. You won't have trouble with that, except it isn't hung on fences here like it is in Norway."

Kristian took another drink of his coffee and chuckled as he added . . . "and then you'll have to milk cows!"

Ole already had been helping his cousins with the milking and had discovered some muscles in his wrists and arms he hadn't used before. Milking was a woman's task in Norway.

Kristian went on, ". . . and you'll have to haul bundles and help with threshing . . . and pick corn, besides the plowing. There is plenty to do on a Dakota farm."

Ole listened carefully and seriously announced, "*I am willing to work.*"

"Yah, you have Lundby blood in you," Aunt Berte reminded Ole. "Your Grandpa Lundby was one of the finest farmers in Hurdal, and you'll do all right, too. Lundby descendants are born farmers. You'll learn the Dakota ways."

July came to Norway Township, and days for the farm families were long and arduous. The green fields of wheat and oats had headed, and soon the grain would begin to turn golden. The first cutting of hay had now been taken care of, and Ole Nordlie had had a chance to experience the Dakota heat as his assignment had been to stand in the stack and arrange the hay into a well-shaped mound on the hottest day so far this summer.

On the 7th of July, welcome showers came and the milking and other chores were finished early. Now Ole would have time to write a letter home. He could not forget the goodbye the day he left Hurdal or the promise he made to his mother to write faithfully. Already, it had been over a month since his last letter.

He began . . .

July 7, 1888

"*Kjaere* Mother,

How is it with you and the family? I hope you are all well. I want you to know everything is fine with me. I have a good place to work here in America and am learning how to be a farmer in the New Country.

It has been raining here today and I haven't had much to do so I have had time to think about you and *Nordlien*. Have you put up the hay yet? Do you have plenty of help? Is brother Ludvig still at home?

Today I have been remembering Pa. It was two years ago today that he died. I'm sure you had thoughts of him today also. How things have changed from that day!

I suppose Gunda has been up at the *seter* at Snultra with the cows for several weeks already."

Ole stopped a moment to reflect. It was up at Snultra a year ago when he had first been confronted with the suggestion he should leave *Nordlien*. Then the letter had come from Auntie Grue in Dakota. And now he was here. But during these last hot sultry days his thoughts had gone back to the beautiful cool Hurdal valley.

After this year Mother had promised to turn *Nordlien* over to brother Laurits, who had the "*odelsret.*" But what would happen to Mother and the girls? Ole was concerned for them. Would Laurits look after them? He had his own family to care for.

Ole returned again to his letter . . .

"The latest news is that Aunt Berte and the family may be moving. Kristian and Ole Hagbart are now on a trip up farther north about one hundred fifty miles where there is land to get. If they find some, I promised I would help them move next spring.

You probably wonder what this land in Dakota looks like. It is hard for me to describe so you can picture it in your mind. I would say it is generally rather flat, and there are no mountains to look up to. I guess I miss the beauty and the comfort of the mountains more than anything else.

I must tell you that all the people around here are from Norway so I don't feel like I am in a foreign land. Only when we go to town there are certain stores run by Americans where Norwegian is not understood.

I must close for now. Greet little Mathilda, and Ingeborg and Ludvig."

Ole was about to sign his name and close his letter, but a feeling of guilt jabbed him. After a short debate with himself, he dipped his pen, swallowed hard and added . . .

"Greet brother Laurits and Karine and baby."

Love, your son,
Ole"

Chapter V

Norway Township in Lincoln County, Dakota Territory had come a long way in the twenty years since it had first been homesteaded. Norwegians who had settled this area had been joined by more relatives, friends and countrymen. The community was a little bit of the Fatherland, with its Norwegian customs and language.

The cottonwood saplings the early pioneers had planted on the bare prairie were beginning to emerge as groves. The sod huts and shanties they had first built now stood in the background on some farms as fine frame houses were being constructed.

The settlers who began with a team of oxen now owned horses or mules, and the number of their other livestock had increased.

Schools had been built every three or four miles. The Norwegian language was used in the homes and churches, but in the schools English was required.

Three Norwegian churches had been established in the community and for most of these hard working people their lives revolved around their homes and their churches.

Well-travelled paths between farms spoke of the strong bonds of friendship which existed between neighboring families after having weathered the bad and good times together.

Norwegian newcomers were arriving all the time. They worked on the farms as hired men and hired girls. Here they learned the ways of the New Country and often married and remained.

Many of the pioneers with their large families now had their children married and living in the community. But the generation of children born of the Norwegian immigrants did not have the same love and memories of Norway their parents had.

On November 2, 1889, Dakota Territory was admitted into the Union as two states—North Dakota and South Dakota. Norway Township in Lincoln County now became part of South Dakota. And on that day all the people living in these two states became United States citizens, including a young man from Hurdal, Norway, named Ole Christian Nordlie.

Friday evening, December 5th, 1889, was the date set for the Lands Ladies Aid auction at the Rise schoolhouse. Members had been knitting and sewing all year, preparing articles for this event. It was a social gathering all of the community living in the northern part of Norway Township attended.

"Will you go with?" Stener Paulson questioned his hired man, Ole Nordlie.

"Yah, Nordlie, you should go," coaxed motherly Thora Paulson. "There will be many pairs of hand-knit woolen stockings for sale—and mittens too! You could use some now when you are picking corn in this cold weather."

"Oh, I suppose I can go," Nordlie agreed.

The cold weather had begun, and that evening Stener Paulson tucked his family in the buggy with lap robes and loaded Thora's contributions for the sale in a box in the rear of the buggy. Nordlie rode beside Stener.

When they arrived at the schoolhouse, it was buzzing with activity. The ladies were hanging up their articles—knit stockings, mittens and caps, aprons, and crocheted doilies. On the teacher's desk were cakes and other baked goods. Because there had been school, the stove had been burning all day and the room was comfortable.

The men and boys stood in the rear of the schoolroom visiting while the women prepared for the event.

Ole Nordlie joined several other newcomers and was listening to their conversation when one of the men of the community approached him.

"Are you Nordlie?" the man asked.

"Yes, sir," Ole Nordlie responded.

The man explained that he was Ole Overseth who lived about a mile southeast of the schoolhouse.

Nordlie looked him over. He appeared to be in his forties, with a full beard and a pleasant, cheerful manner.

Ole Overseth came right to the point, "Well, then you're the one I want! I hear you've had experience plowing up sod."

"Well, yes," Nordlie answered, a little surprised a stranger knew something about him. "This summer up in Day County I helped break up the prairie for my cousins who moved there."

"I am looking for someone I can hire to turn up sod on several quarters of land I purchased several years ago just west of Eden. Much of it hasn't been plowed yet. Have you taken on a job for next year?" Ole Overseth questioned.

"When the cornpicking is finished at Stener Paulsons, I have nothing more lined up."

"If you are interested," Overseth proposed, and gave Nordlie a kindly smile, "you can just as well come to my place when you finish at Stener's. I have a lot of livestock and could use another man during the winter months."

The first week in January, 1890, Ole Nordlie began his employment for Ole Overseth. The Overseth farm was a busy place, even in winter. With many horses, milk cows and hogs to care for besides feeder cattle, the days were filled with hard labor. On cold winter days, the ice had to be chopped out of the tank, hay hauled, and often snow needed to be shovelled so the animals could get to their feed.

The winter days were short, but the winter nights were long. The kitchen was the gathering place after supper, where the cook stove with its open oven door made the room warm and cozy.

Ole Overseth's oldest son, Johnny, almost sixteen, had finished country school, and now was helping his father with the farm work. Tonight he sat at the kitchen table with paper and pencil, trying to figure prices on feeder cattle, to see if he could estimate the amount of profit when they would be sold.

Martin, now nine, also sat at the kitchen table. He held his hands over his ears to keep out the conversations in the room while he concentrated on the material he would be tested over at school the next day. Recently he had been given an incentive for good grades from Uncle Pete, his father's brother, who had promised to give him his cornet and teach him to play it . . . provided he received a good report from the school.

Christian Narum, Mrs. Overseth's bachelor brother, leaned his chair backwards and lazily smoked his pipe. His task in the Overseth home was to keep a supply of wood for the stoves. This was a full time job.

Ole Nordlie re-read the Norwegian paper he had studied the night before. He picked up the "*Sioux Valley News*" and glanced through that, but there were only a few words there he could understand.

Little Anna Overseth, who was in the first grade at the Rise School, came into the kitchen with her Reader. She brought it to Christian and addressed him with this request, "Uncle Chris, will you hear my lesson?"

Christian continued leaning backwards in his chair, sleepily enjoying the stove's warmth as he now and then took a puff of his pipe. Finally he answered, "Yah, what is it you want?"

Anna moved closer and repeated her request,

"Will you hear my lesson? I have to give it by memory at school tomorrow. Please?"

Christian softened at her "Please," but he was so comfortable. "*Aw, Vesla* (little one), can't you see I am smoking my pipe?" Then a thought came to him and he suggested, "Have Nordlie listen to you. Why, you can help him learn English."

Ole Nordlie, who sat at the kitchen table, heard Christian's remarks. He liked books, and thought this was his opportunity. Oh, if only he could learn to read English!

"Come here, and show me your book," he invited.

Anna opened her Primer to the poem she was learning. On the page was a picture of a kitten.

"You explain the words to me first," Ole said. He pointed to each word as Anna translated it to him in Norwegian.

" 'I', that is '*jeg*'," Anna explained, "and 'love' is '*elske*'." " 'Little' must be '*liten*'," Nordlie interrupted, 'but 'Pussy' . . . what is that?"

"Oh, you know, '*kattunge*' (kittens)." They followed through the poem, word by word.

Ole Nordlie was enjoying this project. Many times he had helped his little sister Mathilda with her schoolwork, and Anna reminded him of her.

"All right, now say it all for me, and I'll follow along in your book," instructed Nordlie.

Anna cleared her throat and recited the poem she would give in school the next day:

Pussy

I love little pussy
Her fur is so warm
And if I don't hurt her
She'll do me no harm.

I'll pet little pussy
And then she will purr
And show me her thanks
For my kind deeds to her.

"*Akkurat*! Correct!" Ole Nordlie stated.

Anna was pleased Nordlie commended her, and briefly studied this man who was willing to help her with her lesson. "Do you know any poems, Mr. Nordlie?" she asked.

"Well," Nordlie said, as he thought a moment, "there was one poem I had to learn when I went to school. This poem is famous in my home at Hurdal because a former pastor's wife there wrote it with Hurdal in mind."

"Is it about a cat?" Anna asked.

"*Nei*, it is about a '*budeie*'."

Nordlie saw the puzzled expression on her face and went on to explain, "A *budeie* is the dairymaid who takes care of the cows, both winter and summer. It is different in Norway. There the women do that kind of work."

Now five-year-old Tony also had joined Anna.

"I am going to take care of Pa's cows when I get bigger," he explained.

"The name of this poem is — '*The Dairymaid's Song*'," and he began reciting it in Norwegian:

"*The winter is long for those who tend livestock,*
How tedious the work to keep cows fed and clean."

Ole looked at his little audience to see if they were listening. Two pairs of eyes were upon him as he continued.

"*Cold and snowflakes will definitely not scare me.*
Yea, though icicles hang from the hem of my skirt."

The children giggled at the thought of that.

"*It always is cozy in the barn in the evening*
And those who are tired sleep well under the sheepskin."

"You see, in Norway many *budeie* have a bed upstairs in the barn where they sleep," Nordlie pointed out.

Nordlie went on as if he was a preacher preaching to his congregation,

"BUT THERE SHALL BE SPRING when the neckyokes we loosen
Then all the young cattle will bound out of the barn.

The cows will toss their heads and make a spectacle
And sniff and stare, as they notice Spring's miracle.
Then I shall to the *seters* willingly bring myself,
Where I will tend the cows, make cheese and churn."

"What is a *seter*?" Anna asked.

"Way up on the mountain are pastures of green grass," Ole explained. "Here the dairymaid takes the cows in the summertime."

"We don't have any mountains," Tony complained.

"When I return home with the wooden pails brimful
At the farm I will be greeted by the girls and the boys.
The cows will bellow for they know they are home again,
And I will be treated as if I'm a guest."

Nordlie had to explain this event for the children.

"In late August or September, it is time to bring the cattle back home to the barn. They are chased down from the *seters*, and they are so happy to be home again. There is much excitement as the *budeie* reaches the farm; the little boys and girls run to meet the procession. The poem ends like this:

"Yah, lucky the one who a herd can own,
But since I have no farm, I will be *a dairymaid*!"

He repeated the last two lines,

"Yah, lucky the one who a herd can own,
But since I have no farm, I will be . . ."

He paused a moment and added . . .

"I will be *a HIRED MAN*!"

"Oh, that's a good story," exclaimed Tony.

"Children," their mother, Johanna Overseth, called from the sitting room. "It's time for devotions and bedtime."

"You can come too." Anna grabbed Nordlie's hand and pulled him along into the other room. Here the rest of the family was gathered.

Father Ole Overseth sat in the rocking chair holding two-year-old Jim, who had fallen asleep. In the cradle, baby Henry was also sleeping.

The oldest daughter of the family, Helmina, was seated by the lamp with her knitting in her lap. She was thirteen years, going on fourteen. Her heavy brown hair was brushed back from her forehead and tucked behind her ears so it hung down her back. Both Helmina and her mother had been working on mittens for the children in the family.

John and Martin sat down on the floor. Uncle Christian had decided to go to bed.

"Mama, Nordlie has been telling us about the girl who takes care of the cows up on the *seters*," Anna informed her mother.

Johanna Overseth helped Tony climb into her lap, and then she responded.

"You say you have been hearing about the one who takes care of the cows?"

She paused a moment and then she announced, "Well, tonight let's read about the One who takes care of the sheep."

Johanna reached for her Bible which lay on the table and leafed through the pages until she found John 10. She cleared her voice and began to slowly read verse 14:

"I am the Good Shepherd; I know my sheep. And they know me."

She finished with a prayer and after they had sung a hymn, Johanna instructed the little ones to get to bed.

As Nordlie arose to retire, Ole Overseth called after him.

"Would you get the team ready for me early in the morning? Tomorrow I have to go to Canton with the wagon."

Nordlie went upstairs to the hired men's room where Christian was already snoring. He quickly undressed in the chilly temperature, then crawled under the heavy quilts. As he lay there, his thoughts went over the evening—Anna's poem, the new English words.

Yah, and to think he had still remembered Hannah Vinsness' poem he had learned back at Erikstellet School. His thoughts went back to Hurdal. He wondered how his mother and sisters were tonight. Were they warm and well? Was Laurits keeping Mother supplied with plenty of wood?

As he drifted off to sleep, the words Mrs. Overseth had read ran through his mind—*"I know my sheep. And they know Me."*

He sleepily pondered this. Yes, he was aware Jesus knew the ones who were His, but the last part of the verse intrigued him . . . *"and they know Me."* He would really like to get TO KNOW HIM better.

The next morning Ole Nordlie was up earlier than usual. It was a pleasant winter day, a nice day for a trip to Canton.

While Johnny was busy with the cattle, Ole Nordlie watered and fed the horses. In winter, the horses' hair tended to be thick and unruly, so he took time to groom them. They must look shiny and sleek when they were going to town. Nordlie then harnessed them.

While working with the horses, his thoughts returned to that day almost three years ago, the year before he came to America. He remembered it so well. He had just finished currying the horses and had the harnesses on them when his brother had come to take over the team and wagon.

That was the day Ole Nordlie knew there wasn't room for both Laurits and him at *Nordlien*.

Ole still could hear his mother as she later spoke to them about the matter.

"Oh, my boys! Now that your father is gone, we must work together. Will you be like Jacob and Esau, always quarreling over each other's rights?"

Now, three years later in South Dakota of America, Ole Nordlie considered her statement.

"Yah, just call me Ole JACOB," Ole said to himself. He had left home even as Jacob had. Now he was in the far away country working as a hired man like Jacob did. And he missed his mother, and his sisters, brother Ludvig, and the *Nordlien* farm . . . and Hurdal. Though he didn't like to admit it, at times he even missed Laurits. But the hurt his brother had caused him still hadn't gone away.

Suddenly Ole Nordlie was brought back to the present.

"Is the team ready?" called Overseth.

"Yes sir, I'll have them right out. It will only take five minutes to hitch them to the wagon."

Chapter VI

Johanna Overseth untied Nancy, her horse, from the hitching post by the Lands Church. It was a pleasant April day in 1893. She had spent the afternoon across the road at the new parsonage, visiting with the young pastor's wife, Emma Hauge.

First, Johanna had gone to the Moe Post Office at the Hanson farm and picked up the mail; then she had stopped at the Hauges with butter, eggs and some lefse she had baked that morning. The Pastor's wife had been doing spring housecleaning, but she had insisted that Johanna come in and have some coffee.

As Johanna climbed into the buggy and turned her horse eastward for the two-and-one-half miles home, she glanced again at the parsonage and felt pride at the fine new home the Lands and Eden congregations had erected for their pastor and his bride. It stood square in proportions and two stories tall.

As her horse trotted along, Johanna had many things to think about. The Pastor's wife was so young . . . just out of high school, and so lonesome. Johanna was glad she had spent some time with her. The Hauges had been married for almost a year now, but it would be better when they had a family. Then she wouldn't be so lonesome. She had come from the town of Estherville, Iowa, and wasn't accustomed to this quiet country life.

When Johanna reached the mile corner, she pulled on the right rein to turn Nancy south, although she imagined the horse knew very well they were heading home.

Again, Johanna's thoughts went back to her visit. Out loud she muttered "*Stukkers jente!*" (Poor girl!) as she recalled Emma telling of her fear when she saw the two strangers entering their barn early one evening. And the Pastor wasn't even home! The young Pastor's wife had been so terrified she had hidden in the clothes closet until the Pastor returned. The two men had been traveling on foot and had only wanted a place to sleep. But what was a young lady to think? She was barely twenty years old. Why, she was only three years older than daughter Helmina!

Fru Hauge that afternoon had shown Johanna the blueprints Pastor Hauge had drawn for a fine new altar for the Lands Church. It would make the church so *festlig*, Johanna decided. Since the second Lands Church had been erected over twelve years ago, no new church furnishings had been added. The settlers had gotten along with the bare necessities. And he had drawn plans for a pulpit too. Yes, it was good to have young and creative ideas in the church. God's house should be beautiful.

But what had surprised Johanna most this afternoon was when Fru Hauge had asked her if Nordlie, their hired man, had decided to take charge of the Sunday School this year. Why, she had heard him say nothing about that. But it was good that Pastor Hauge had asked him because Nordlie was capable. Still, it wasn't like Nordlie to push himself into the foreground.

Last year Hauge had Jens Bjorlie, another newcomer, organize a Sunday School at Lands. Bjorlie had found several others to help him teach the classes, and Nordlie was one. In the fall they had ended with a big Sunday School and Choral Fest. This year Bjorlie had given up the Sunday School work, because after all, he was a musician, and he had many choirs in the community to direct.

Again, Nancy had come to an intersection and Johanna now directed her horse east until they would reach the driveway to home.

Yah, it was a pleasant surprise that Pastor wanted Nordlie to lead the Sunday School this year. She must encourage him to do so. They must keep the Sunday School going.

Then she remembered that in the mail was a letter from Norway for Nordlie. She was anxious to have the men come in for supper so she could surprise him with it. Letters from Norway pleased him so much.

Johanna left her horse with brother Christian to unharness and hurried into the house. This afternoon daughter Helmina had been baking cookies while looking after her brothers, four-year-old Henry and five-year-old Jim. Now Helmina stood at the stove stirring the rice porridge they would have for supper.

On the table stood stacks of sugar cookies that daughter Anna was putting into the large round wooden cookie box. The two little boys, Henry and Jim, were beside her, standing on tip-toes, little beggars waiting for the broken pieces. Upon seeing their mother, they ran to her, each boy grabbing a leg.

Trumpet blasts were coming from upstairs. "I sent Martin to his room to practice his horn," Helmina explained. "It was just too much '*spetakkel*' (racket) down here."

"Yah, it is hard to know what to do. It seems like music is all Martin is interested in. And Pa is so proud he is picking up the cornet so fast. After it gets warmer, Martin will have to practice outside. That's all there is to it!"

Johanna broke away from the little boys and went to change her clothes. When she came back to the kitchen, the girls had set the table, and the men had come in for supper. Johanna presented Nordlie his letter from Norway, and he slipped it into his back pocket.

Helmina dished up the rice porridge. Nordlie watched her as she made the trips back and forth from the stove to the table, setting a bowl at each place. A few curls hanging around her face gave her a soft look and set off her large eyes. Just in the three years he had been there, Helmina had developed from a girl into a fine looking young woman.

Nordlie sprinkled cinnamon and sugar on his rice and took several spoonfuls. Helmina was a good cook. And not a bit lazy. *Nei, langt ifra*! (No, far from it!) Yah, someday she would make some man a fine wife.

During the supper meal Johanna told about her visit at the parsonage and mentioned that Pastor Hauge was trying to get the Sunday School started again. "I hear he would like you to be president this year." Johanna directed that remark at Nordlie.

"It is a big responsibility for a newcomer," was all that he replied.

"Oh, you can do it, Nordlie," said Overseth.

"Yah, you would do a good job," Johanna agreed.

After the supper dishes had been cleared, Helmina and Anna began to wash and dry them. Ole Nordlie had seated himself in the corner of the kitchen and had taken the letter from Norway out of his pocket. He intended to read it but was distracted as he watched the two girls. Helmina, intent on her task, stood with her hands in the dishpan. For a few moments he studied Helmina and then an idea came to him. She would make a good Sunday School teacher. He would speak to her about it. He arose from his chair and approached her.

"Ah-hem, Helmina," he spoke up.

Helmina was startled at the interruption, and a faint blush crept over her face. Helmina was now sixteen years of age. In June she would reach seventeen. She stood there with rolled-up sleeves and wet hands and attempted to push back the strands of hair that had fallen over her eyes.

Nordlie cleared his throat and went on, "Helmina, I was wondering if you would help me if I take the Sunday School job. The thought came to me that you and Minnie Sogn would be good teachers for the little folks. You would be teaching them Bible stories — just like you do Henry and Jim."

For a few moments Helmina continued washing the dishes. Finally she raised her eyes.

"Well, if you think I can do it," she timidly replied, and added, "I think Minnie would help."

Now he had taken the first step in the Sunday School undertaking. He again sat down in the corner of the kitchen and opened his letter from Norway. It was from his sister Ingeborg.

"Dear Brother,

You may not have heard that I am now in Østre Toten. After my training in Christiania, I took a position at the large Sullestad *"gaard"* near Lake Mjøsa. Life and farming here in Toten is on a bigger scale. There is much more tillable land here than the little patches on the mountainsides at Hurdal. They raise wheat, barley and potatoes, and from the window I can see Lake Mjøsa.

It takes a lot of work to keep the many laborers on the farm fed and the large house clean. Several other girls work with me. We do a lot of baking. I have learned to make *totenkringler*, a sweet roll that is a Toten specialty. A friend from Hurdal, Otto Rognlien, has been up to visit me several times and this keeps me from getting too lonely.

The last time I was home to visit, Mother reported that all was well. The big house has been divided so Mother has a few rooms of her own for privacy, and Laurits and Karine and family have the rest. Now that Mother is alone most of the time, she really doesn't need much room.

You know what a worker Mother is. She still is busy. Before Christmas, it was Mother who did the butchering as usual. If she can't find anything else to do, she is scrubbing her wooden floors and walls. She isn't one to sit in the rocking chair and do embroidery.

Mathilda has finished school now and has been having some jobs working in homes when extra help is needed. Ludvig is working in Toten on one of these large farms here.

We all miss you and hope everything is well with you. Write when you can.

Love,
Ingeborg"

That night as Ole Nordlie retired, he had many things to turn over in his mind. Getting the Sunday School organized really weighed on him. He didn't want to take on a job if he couldn't do it well. But it must not interfere with his hired man's duties.

He clasped his hands together and turned to the Lord, *"Fader vor"* (Our Father), If you will help me, I will take the Sunday School job."

After all, the Lord had promised guidance, and a newcomer from Norway really needed that! His thoughts now went back to Norway, and he asked God's blessing on his mother and brothers and sisters there.

Later that summer, in the July 28th, 1893 issue of the Lincoln County newspaper, the following article appeared in the Norway Township column:

"The Sunday School is progressing finely under the able management of O. Nordlie as President. The attendance is about seventy, and the assistant teachers are Mrs. H. K. Rise, Miss Overseth, Miss Sogn and Gunda Jacobson."

When fall came, Nordlie and the teachers considered ways to end the Sunday School year. A choral fest like last year was out of the question. One of the teachers had heard of the Christmas programs that city churches had begun to present. "Yah, that sounds like a good idea," Nordlie agreed. Christmas was what Sunday School was all about, and with the good attendance they had, they could produce a fine program for the parents and other church members. Plans were immediately put into action for this new event.

"We'll have to take both buggies tonight," Ole Overseth announced.

"Nordlie, you take Helmina, Anna, Martin and Tony with you since you all have to be there early."

It was Christmas Day evening, 1893, the night of the first Sunday School Christmas program at the Lands Church. Since Nordlie was President of the Sunday School and Helmina one of the teachers, it was necessary they get there and see that everything was in order before folks began to arrive.

Nordlie had been tense all day. He wasn't good at trying new things. Perhaps people wouldn't come after all the practicing and work the teachers and he had been through. Well, anyway, he told himself, he hoped the parents would be there and the Christmas story would be told.

The little church soon filled with many people, both downstairs and in the balcony. The teachers had tried to decorate a little with a few evergreen boughs and ribbons, because they hadn't gotten permission to have a Christmas tree. The lamps had been lit, and there was an excitement in the air. Something new was about to happen.

When it was time to begin, Nordlie stood up and welcomed the audience. He opened his Bible to Luke 2:5 and read the invitation...*"Come, let us go to Bethlehem and see this thing which has come to pass, which the Lord has made known to us."* He paused a moment and added, "It is the wish of the teachers and the children that the first Christmas will come alive for us all tonight.

"Now, let us begin by singing together '*Et Barn er Fodt i Bethlehem*' (A Babe is Born in Bethlehem)."

Nordlie motioned for Minnie Sogn to begin playing the pump organ, and Jens Bjorlie stood up and placed his violin in position. As the music began, Nordlie faced the audience and led in the singing.

> *"A babe is born in Bethlehem,*
> *in Bethlehem;*
> *Therefore rejoice Jerusalem.*
> *Hal-le-lu-jah! Hal-le-lu-jah!"*

Ole Nordlie watched the people as they sang this familiar Christmas carol in their native tongue. Even up in the balcony where many of the newcomers and bachelors sat, he noticed the enthusiasm of their singing.

He glanced at all the Sunday School children, their eyes sparkling with the excitement of this night. There sat Carl, who would probably be too bashful to speak up when it was his turn, and the Ekle boys with their fine voices and the little Sogn girl with the lamplight shining on her golden hair.

Looking across the audience, his eyes rested on Stener Paulson and his wife, at whose farm he had worked as a hired man several years ago, Lars and Maria Sogn, and Ole and Johanna Overseth, where he was now employed. Most of them seemed to know all of the verses by heart.

"Hal-le-lu-jah! Hal-le-lu-jah!"

It was good to be there among these familiar faces. And a fact hit him. This community in Norway Township in Nordamerica was beginning to feel like home.

Helmina Overseth and youngest brother, Henry — Circa 1894.

Chapter VII

The March wind was cold and raw. Ole Nordlie had tried to keep his back to it as much as possible. Yah, it was true as Hannah Vinsness had written, *"The winter is long for those who tend livestock."* It meant so much extra work, trudging through snow, hauling water and feed. Almost endless labor.

The Overseth farm had greatly expanded its cattle-feeding operation. Now in the winter of 1894 there seemed to be cattle everywhere. Early last fall, two long wooden frames had been built at right angles and covered with straw at threshing time. With openings only to the south and east, the animals could go in there and find protection from the north wind. It provided a good shelter during the winter months.

Today Overseth, his son Johnny, and Nordlie had been working among the cattle, sorting out the choicest head, the ones ready for market. These they had corralled into a separate enclosure. These sixty head would fill three cars on the train that would be heading for Chicago in two days. Tomorrow a cattle drive would chase these fat steers to the Hudson depot. This was the same depot where Nordlie had arrived six years ago when he had come from Norway. Several years ago the town of Eden had changed its name to Hudson, so it was no longer called the Eden depot.

Ole Nordlie was excited and pleased Overseth had had enough confidence in his son Johnny and him to put them in charge of the cattle on the three-day train trip to the stockyards in Chicago. This time Ole Overseth wasn't traveling along. He had many projects going here in South Dakota. These past two months they had been hauling stones and lumber for the gigantic barn Overseth would erect in the summer. Also, Overseth was making arrangements for the remaining calves and feeder cattle. In about a month these would be shipped west by train to the ranch Ole

Byhre managed near Presho. Yes, there was much activity at the Overseth farm this year.

When the evening chores were finished, Nordlie was tired. The cold wind and the hard day's work made him look forward to a warm place and a good hot meal.

Overseth, Johnny and Nordlie headed for the house. Nordlie and Johnny carried along the pails of milk from the evening milking. Inside the door they pulled off their boots, heavy jackets and scarves. They were greeted by little five-year-old Henry.

"Brrr-rr, it's cold outside! Close the door!" he told them. Then little Henry began to giggle and point at his father and Nordlie. "You are icicle men!"

As the men came into the kitchen they were welcomed by the smell of coffee and cooking foods. Then Nordlie glanced into the mirror hanging above the wash basin. Numerous icicles were hanging from his mustache. It was kind of funny but his cheeks were so cold it was hard to smile. He brushed the icicles from his mustache, then washed his face and with a towel rubbed warmth back into his cheeks.

Well, icicles go with winter. Nordlie knew that. He wasn't a stranger to winter weather. Memories of his younger days included the long winters of Hurdal. He looked into the mirror again and wondered if it would be better if he shaved off his mustache. He couldn't decide if it protected him from the cold or if it made him colder with all the icicles that formed on it.

Johanna Overseth had cooked *lapskaus* for supper. The hot meat and potato stew was just what was needed to warm the men after a chilly day outside.

These days Johanna was very busy because her dependable helper, daughter Helmina, was attending Augustana College in Canton. With the little boys, Henry and Jim, still not in school, they seemed always to be underfoot on these cold days when it was too chilly to play outside. She welcomed daughter Anna's assistance after school each day.

This afternoon Johanna had sent her brother Christian over to the Hansons' to get the mail . . . and it included a letter for Nordlie. As soon as Nordlie left the supper table, he opened the envelope. It was from his sister Ingeborg.

Feb. 10, 1894

Dear brother Ole,

We got your Christmas letter, and we all read it when we were together on Christmas Eve. Mother especially misses you at Christmastime.

I have some rather special news for you. I am engaged to be married to Otto Rognlien from Hurdal. I'm sure you remember him. We have been friends for some time. We have set the date of our wedding for June 24th. I already have purchased material, and veiling too, and will begin sewing my wedding dress in my spare time. There is another woman working here who is an excellent seamstress and she has offered to help me.

I plan to quit my job here in Toten the first of June and will go home and help Mother prepare for the wedding. We will have to butcher, and do a lot of baking for the wedding celebration.

I wish you weren't so far away so you could come home for my special day. I am very happy.

Love,
Ingeborg

Nordlie read the letter over again. *Yah, that was some news!*

Nordlie was happy for his sister Ingeborg. Rognlien was a fine, intelligent man. He thought about his sister. She would make a beautiful bride.

Suddenly it dawned on him. He would not be there to see her! He would have to miss this special family happening. His happiness for his sister turned to sadness at the thought of being absent at this event.

Nordlie arose and headed up the stairs to bed. Oh, he would feel better tomorrow. They had a big day ahead of them . . . and then the next day he would be on the train to Chicago.

The special train that left Hudson, South Dakota, Saturday, March 17th, 1894, for the Chicago stockyards, consisted of eleven carloads of Lincoln County cattle. Other Lincoln County men were shipping and traveling along, and the train would stop each day so the men could feed and water the animals.

Nordlie and Johnny spent much of the time in the company of the other men from the community. But there were times when Nordlie sat by himself. And then his mind went back to Ingeborg's letter. A sad feeling filled his heart, the disappointment of missing out on this special family celebration. To Ole Christian Nordlie, his sisters were very special, and to miss Ingeborg's wedding day — that was a disappointment indeed.

One day as he reflected on it, he even considered making the trip back to Norway for the wedding. There was still time to get there. But that was in a weak moment. He knew that would not be a wise move. He had a good job now, and at this time Overseth really needed him. Furthermore, if he spent what he had saved for this trip, when would his dream of having his own farm ever come true? He did not always want to say . . .

"And since I have no farm of my own,
I will be content to be a hired man."

When they reached Chicago Monday morning, most of the cattle sold for four cents a pound, as the prices were low. Yet when he arrived home and handed over the check, Overseth agreed that it was better than expected.

The Sunday after returning from Chicago, Nordlie spent the afternoon home alone. The Overseths were invited to Johanna's sister's family—the Ole Grevlos'.

The coffee pot was simmering on the back of the cookstove and Nordlie poured up a cup of coffee for himself. He got out his writing paper, and the pen and ink, and sat down at the kitchen table. He read Ingeborg's letter again, and then wrote her a letter of congratulations on her upcoming marriage.

"How fine you will look in your wedding dress," he wrote. Then added, *"You can't guess how much I will miss not being there."*

He poured some more coffee, found a sugar lump to go with it, filled his saucer, and took several slurps of the hot liquid. He sat contemplating what he had written. Suddenly an idea came to him. He would send along a letter for Ingeborg's *"forlovede"* (fiance). Otto Rognlien would be his brother-in-law in a few months, and he wanted to keep in touch with the bridal pair. He dipped the pen and wrote . . .

Dear Future Brother-in-Law
I want to send you a few lines also. I have a request I want to ask of you. When you are married, would you please go to Christiania and have a portrait taken of you both, wearing your wedding clothes, so that I, who am so far away, can also see how you were on your wedding day. I would very much like to see Ingeborg in her wedding veil. I know that you love your bride, so perhaps you can also come to have a fondness for me, her brother. This I desire.

of a horse, or perhaps a lamb bleating for its mother. On Sundays the folks gathered in the Lands or Trinity churches for Sunday services.

At Lands, Pastor Hauge's altar and pulpit had now been finished and put in place. These had been painted white with gold trim. A large painting of Christ hanging on the cross had been inserted above the altar. The back part of the altarpiece extended up the west wall, and along the sides and top of it many little carved spires pointed upward. It was so large and magnificent it was almost too big for the little church that had been built in 1879.

On June 30, 1895, the Lands church was full. The balcony too. Several men had been appointed ushers, and they took their new duties very seriously. Johnny Overseth was one of them.

Pastor L. J. Hauge looked out across his congregation and announced, "Today we shall read from Lukas Evangelium (Gospel), chapter 14, verses 28 and 29:

"Which of you, intending to build, sitteth not down first, and counteth the cost, whether he have sufficient to finish it? Lest haply after he hath laid the foundation and is not able to finish it, all that behold it begin to mock him."

The people in the audience knew well what he was talking about today. Some of them had sat down to count the cost of building a new house and found they couldn't afford it, so they had just added on a room to the old one. No one wanted only a foundation sitting unbuilt and be the laughing stock of Norway Township. Yes, the Bible was right; you have to count the cost before you begin a project.

The Pastor went on . . .

"So likewise, whosoever he be of you that forsaketh not all that he hath, he cannot be my disciple."

Pastor Hauge pounded his fist down on his new pulpit and stated . . . "You have to count the cost! The Christian life isn't a haphazard, hit-and-miss thing. You can't say, 'Sunday morning I will live for Jesus but I'll do as I please the rest of the week.' No, it is a decision to follow through that you make only after you have counted the cost."

Ole Nordlie listened intently to the sermon. He understood Pastor Hauge was trying to tell them the Christian life was a total commitment. Nordlie was learning more about the Christian life all the time.

And Ole Nordlie knew about counting the cost. He wanted to buy a farm, but he couldn't pay the price yet. The money came very slowly. He should be getting his share of money soon from his brother Laurits who had taken over *Nordlien*. He was glad the Christian life didn't depend on how much money he had.

Nordlie looked across to the women and children's side of the church and got a quick glimpse of Helmina Overseth. This spring and summer had been happy for Nordlie. He had joined the choir at Helmina's suggestion, and he had the opportunity to take her to choir practice every week. These were nights he looked forward to.

His mind began to wander. This afternoon the Normanna Band boys were giving a special concert in the Rise schoolhouse, and it was announced they would be wearing new uniforms. On this fine summer day, he planned to ask Helmina to walk with him the mile and a half over there for the concert.

Nordlie glanced out the church window. Across the road to the north was the parsonage and today its green lawn was brightened with dandelions, and the sun was shining. *Yah, it was a very fine summer day.*

Chapter IX

The year of 1896 was an election year. *"Free Silver and Bryan"* seemed to be the topic of conversation when two or more people gathered.

William Jennings Bryan was running on the People's party, and Norway Towship was definitely behind him. As the months went by, the tension built. There were meetings in country schoolhouses with enthusiastic speakers proclaiming Free Silver as the farmer's hope for prosperity. No national election before had seen Lincoln County, South Dakota citizens so involved.

The year of 1896 had brought more progress to the enterprising little country corner of Moe. The store now run by Button and his new partner, Oluf Ekle, was having a fine trade. In February the cooperative creamery built in 1895 began production. The first week over 3,000 pounds of milk were taken in and each week showed an increase. Milk was delivered each day to the creamery where its equipment made it into butter, with the buttermilk being returned to the farmers. Osmund Steensland of the Hudson Hardware provided the cans. Ole Overseth furnished the most milk—over forty gallons a day.

Ole Overseth had doubled his herd of milk cows after he became a stockholder. With many young sons growing up and several hired men to do the milking, he felt it was the up-coming progressive way to make money on the farm.

The year of 1896 also happened to be Leap Year, and it would bring Norway Township a number of weddings.

There were many young people in the community, and one activity they were involved in was the Normanna Choir. Every week for several years they had met and practiced under the direction of Jens Bjorlie. They liked to make music, but it was also an important part of their social life; and it was here many love affairs came into bloom.

The first wedding in the community was held on February 26th at the Trinity Church with the Overseth's neighbor, Emma Larsen, marrying Ole Steensland of Highland Township. A reception was held in the home of the bride's parents, Nils and Lisa Larsen. The Overseths, with Helmina and Johnny, attended and presented the bride and groom with a dinner set.

"Mother, I think we're getting company," Helmina called to her mother, Johanna Overseth, who was working in the kitchen.

"It looks like August and Maria," she added.

Helmina was sitting by the south window sewing when she noticed the team of horses and buggy turn up their lane. She was making a dress for her twelve-year-old sister, Anna, to wear for the special event that was approaching.

Johanna hurried to the living room window to look.

"I wonder if Maria has her new baby along."

Johanna hadn't seen her friend since right after the baby girl's birth the last of January, and that was over a month now.

August and Maria Johnson were the Ole Overseth's closest neighbors. They lived about a quarter of a mile east of them on the south side of the road. Both August and Maria had immigrated from Sweden. August was a bachelor when he homesteaded about the time Ole Overseth did. Maria arrived in the United States about ten years later, in 1882. They belonged to the Augustana Synod Trinity Church, which was located northeast of the Overseth farm, while the Overseths were members of the Lands Norwegian Synod Church, two miles to the northwest.

Johanna hurried to the door and opened it for Maria, who had the bundled-up baby in her arms. August followed, carrying little Esther, who was not quite three years old. Maria was a large woman while her husband was of smaller and wirier proportions.

After August got his family inside, he returned to his team and buggy, for he was on his way to the Rise schoolhouse to fetch their two older children, Anna and Hermand, from school.

"It was such a nice March day that I told August I'd ride along and come here while he picked up the children from school. I have hardly been out of the house since the baby was born," Maria explained.

She opened up the blankets that covered the baby's face and then called to her toddler, "Esther, let Johanna help you get your scarf and coat off."

While the women unbundled the children in the kitchen, they visited.

Maria turned to her friend. "Johanna, I just had to come over and find out about all the excitement at your house. Is it all true?"

When Maria had the baby unwrapped, Johanna held her. Johanna looked down at the chubby little face and remarked, "You have such fine looking babies, Maria."

"Yah, that is true, isn't it?" Maria answered with motherly pride. "But *Rute* (Ruth) isn't such a good baby as the others were. I have to get up many times a night with her."

"She will outgrow that, Maria," Johanna advised.

Maria quickly changed the subject. "Now I didn't come here to talk about my children. I want to hear all about the upcoming wedding. Yah, and about your trip to Norway." She lifted little Esther into her lap and added, "This is all so exciting."

Johanna informed her Helmina and Nordlie's wedding would take place in six weeks on April 30th. "That will be on a Thursday—in the Lands Church, of course," she added.

Maria sat and smoothed her little daughter's long hair as she listened. "This wedding was no surprise to me, Johanna. Why last year already, I told August it could well be that Nordlie and Helmina would someday get married. Nordlie is a fine Christian man, Johanna."

"We think so too," Johanna agreed. "It will work out so well for us that now Nordlie and Helmina can stay here while we get to take the trip back to Norway."

The baby was beginning to fuss, so Johanna gently rocked her from side to side.

"I can't wait to see my father again. He is crippled and in bed all the time now."

"Oh, that two such big things should happen at the same time like this must have you busy getting ready."

"Yes, it seems the wedding list is getting longer every day."

"*I hope we will get to come,*" Maria hinted.

"Oh course, Maria. You are our nearest neighbor and one of my special friends."

"Now tell me about the wedding dress," Maria begged.

"Well, I cannot tell you much about that. Next week my Ole will go with Helmina and me to Sioux City on the train. There we will pick out the material and laces and pattern. And we must do other shopping also. If we are going to Norway, we will all need new shoes and Ole plans to buy a new suit."

The baby had closed her eyes so Johanna laid her down on Ole's couch and got out some cups and saucers. She poured up some of the coffee that was keeping hot on the back of the cookstove.

Maria still had more questions to ask. "Tell me then, who will be the attendants?"

"Helmina has asked her friend, Minnie Sogn, and she is also having her childhood friend, Josephine Odegaard. I think Johnny will probably stand up with Nordlie. He just got a new suit for his church ushering job so he won't need to buy another one."

Maria looked down at her toddler. "Yah, if little Esther was older, she could be a flower girl," Maria suggested.

"There won't be any flower girls. Both Nordlie and Helmina want it simple."

Esther got down on the floor and began playing with the cat.

"What August and I have been trying to figure out," Maria questioned, "is where are they going to live?"

"As I mentioned before, they will stay here until we get back from Norway in September. Then we have the other farm down by Eden — er, Hudson, you know," Johanna pointed out.

"I am so glad I am finding out all these things," Maria explained. "I've been so curious."

The two women sat at the table and began to drink their coffee.

"Here, Maria, have a *sukkarbit* with your coffee," Johanna offered.

"Thank you," she said in her Swedish language as she reached for a sugar lump and dipped it into her coffee cup.

"Well, you told me the wedding date, but what date do you sail for Norway?"

"Ole got the tickets the other day. We leave New York on June 6th. We had planned to take both Henry and Jim along, but Jim just doesn't want to go, so Ole only purchased a ticket for Henry.

"By the way, Mari, did you hear that the Ole Rossums were going to Norway too? They are taking their Emma along. We are all sailing on the same Atlantic steamship on June 6th. And the same thing is happening at the Rossum's as here. Their Mattie will marry Gunder Schiager on May 20th. Helmina heard that Mattie was busy sewing too — both for her wedding, and clothes for her mother and sister's Norway trip. They plan to be gone almost a whole year, but we'll be back in about three months.

Johanna took a drink of her coffee and reflected . . . "The time will go fast from now on. There are so many things to do. When we get back from Sioux City, Maggie Sorlie will be coming over to begin sewing

Helmina's wedding dress. That will be the middle of next week. She'll be here for several weeks—maybe a month—because I need several dresses for my trip to Norway too. And in about a month we will have to butcher because we want fresh beef for the wedding dinner. This will mean putting up meat and all the work that goes with that.

"Oh, Johanna, you mustn't keep on now so you get sick," Maria warned.

"Helmina is such good help, I am sure we will get everything done on time. My sister Helmine will be coming from Minneapolis the week before the wedding to help us, and sister Klara has promised to help with the baking. You can pray for us, though, Maria. We will need some extra strength and wisdom."

Maria arose and as she headed for the living room, she remarked, "I must go in and congratulate the bride-to-be before I leave. August will be coming soon, and he will be in a hurry because he has a good amount of chores to do."

The following Monday, March 23rd, Ole Overseth, Johanna and daughter, Helmina, took the train from Hudson to Sioux City to do their shopping. Helmina found some silk repp fabric in a soft plum color and the prettiest dress pattern, together with white lace for trims and for veiling, artificial white flowers for the crown of the veil and long white elbow-length gloves. They stayed overnight and returned the next day on the afternoon train from Sioux City with all of their purchases.

Meanwhile on Monday, Nordlie was left home alone. Johnny had gone to Moe with the milk, and he planned to spend some time visiting. The daily chores had been taken care of until evening milking. The children wouldn't be home from school for several hours, so Nordlie decided it was a good time to write a letter to his Mother.

March 23, 1896

Kjaere Mor,

Thank you for your Christmas letter. I am so happy every time I hear that you are well. It has been almost eight years now since I left Hurdal, and I suppose there are getting to be many changes there.

I am writing today especially to tell you there will be some changes for me too. Yes, in about six weeks your son Ole Christian shall be married. In my letters I have from time to time mentioned the Overseth's oldest daughter Helmina. Well, she will become my bride on April 30th. She is almost twenty years old, but very mature for her age. She is a fine young lady in every way. I know you would like her, Mother.

My only regret is that neither you, nor any of my family can be here for this special day. You can be sure we will have pictures taken in our wedding clothes and I will send you a picture so you can see the bridal pair.

I was so disappointed Ingeborg and Otto couldn't get to a photographer so I could see them in their wedding clothes.

Some day, as soon as financially possible, I will bring Helmina back to Norway to meet you all.

How is sister Mathilda? I remember the day I left Hurdal I told her some day I'd come back and take her to America. Tell her there are several fine young men in the community who are looking for wives. Perhaps she should think of coming over now if someone from Hurdal makes the trip. Greet her and the rest of the family.

The next time I write I will no longer be an *"ungkar"* (bachelor), but will be a bridegroom.

Take care of yourself, Mother.

Love,
Ole

Ole addressed an envelope, folded his letter and put it inside. He wondered how his mother would feel when she opened it and read he was getting married.

Now Nordlie went to the cookstove and poured up a cup of coffee for himself. Next he took several slips of paper from his pocket. On them were written some sentences. He had been working on a poem to be sung at the bridal dinner. This was a Norwegian custom. Helmina's Uncle Pete Overseth was preparing a speech on behalf of her family. Nordlie had to finish this and get it printed so everyone would have a copy that day.

It was something Ole Nordlie wanted to do. He could not buy his bride a large diamond or strings of pearls, but he would present this poem as a gift of love to her. A lot of time had been spent on it already. He looked through his notes again. He had decided the melody to be used would be *"Blandt alle lande."* He hummed through the melody.

Lately Ole had been thinking about how his Mother had likened his brother and him to Jacob and Esau when they had been quarreling back on the Nordlien farm in Hurdal. Nordlie now considered how similar his life had been to Jacob's. They both had left home and gone to a far country. They both had found work on a farm. They both had fallen in love with the farmer's lovely daughter. However, he was glad to say that he did not have to work seven years without pay for his wife.

Nordlie had decided the first verse would mention this similarity . . .

BRIDEGROOM'S SONG

I crossed the ocean and searched the West
To find the "jente" (girl) I seemed the best.
She is my RACHEL, so fair and shy,
Ole JACOB am I.

Next he would write about how special she was . . .

I love her smile and gentle heart.
I'm thankful today I can be a part
Of all her tomorrows and future days.
I will love her always.

Now he would make his promises to her . . .

I'll give my strength and live my life
To try to bring happiness to my wife.
Through storm and sunshine I'll be by her side,
My lovely bride.

Nordlie thought about the things Helmina and he had discussed — how they both wanted to have a Christian home. He decided he would finish with that thought . . .

Dear God, I thank you for leading me
To this great day of jubilee.
Together we'll serve You, this we a-vow,
In the future and now.

Ole Nordlie spent some time thinking over his situation. It was quite a responsibility he was taking on — getting a wife — and he only a hired man. But his plans did not include always being a hired man! And he felt fortunate to have gotten such a jewel for a wife. Again Nordlie re-read the last verse, and this time he prayed it . . .

"Dear God, I thank you for leading me
To this great day of jubilee.
Together we'll serve You, this we a-vow,
In the future and now.
　　Help me be a kind husband and a good provider.

　　　　　　　　　　　Amen."

Mr. and Mrs. Ole Nordlie, wedding date, April 30, 1896.

Chapter X

"**H**elmina, come and see the paper," Anna called. "The write-up of your wedding is in it."

Helmina hurried to the kitchen. The May 8, 1896 copy of the *Dakota Farmers Leader* had arrived. Martin had brought back the mail when he delivered the milk to the Moe Creamery.

There it was on the back page of the issue, alongside the rural community news columns. The headline read "*The Nordlie-Overseth Wedding.*" Anna laid the paper on the table and both Anna and Helmina tried to read it at the same time. The article began:

> "*Married, Thursday, April 30, 1896, at Lands Church, Rev. L. J. Hauge officiating, Mr. Ole Nordlie to Miss Helmine Overseth.*
> Again the wedding bells rang out joyously over an event which was not entirely unexpected, and about 100 invited guests, relatives and immediate friends of the high contracting parties were called to witness the ceremony which united for life two of the most highly respected parties in Norway township. The bride was attended by Misses Mina Sogn and Josephine Odegaard, and John Overseth and C. T. Hegness acted as groomsmen. The bride, who in her bridal costume presented a most charming appearance, is the daughter of Mr. and Mrs. Ole Overseth."

Helmina felt uncomfortable as she read on, for the editor had included words of praise for both Nordlie and her . . . "*a highly refined and cultured young lady, unusually well qualified to make a model wife and pleasant home,*" and of Nordlie he had written . . . "*industrious and of good morals and excellent habits and held in the highest estimation by all.*"

She finished reading . . .

"After the ceremony in the church had taken place, the guests drove to the residence of the bride's parents where a sumptuous wedding dinner was served in honor of the newly married couple. The neighbors, friends and relatives of Mr. and Mrs. Nordlie all join and wish them all possible joy and prosperity on their journey through life in their new relationship. The following is a list of presents with the names of the donors:

Ole Overseth and wife $100; P. A. Overseth, $50; Hans Overseth, $10; Hans Rise and family, $4; John Hegness and wife, $5; Chas. Johnson, $5; Nels Larson and wife, $4; Halvor Rogness and family, $5; Hans Narum and wife, $3; Paul Gubbrud and wife, $3; H. P. Hanson and wife, $2; Christian Narum, $2; L. H. Sogn and wife, $2; Wm. Odegaard, $2; Ovald Ekle, $2; Jacob, Knute, Gunda and Rena Jacobson, $3; Adolph Gubbrud, $4; Claus, Albert, Oluf and Helmer Hegness, $5; A. Lyngved, $4; Miss Milda Hanson, $4; Theo. Gubbrud, $2; Miss Lorina Wilson, one-half dozen napkins; Aug. Johnson and wife, one tablecloth; Mrs. C. Christopherson and family, silver fruit dish; M. Grevlos, half dozen silver teaspoons; Miss Kaisa Eliason, half dozen cups and saucers; Gust Bergstrom, half dozen knives and forks; John Overseth, one album; O. E. Rossum and family, parlor lamp; John Johnson, silver vegetable dish; Miss Helmine Narum, half dozen of each of silver knives, forks and teaspoons; Miss Minnie Sogn, tablecloth; J. B. Bjorlie, silver spoonholder; Ole Grevlos, half dozen knives and forks; S. K. Tverberg, table cover; Ole Steensland and wife, set of sad irons; Mrs. Sundberg, two flower vases and fresh flowers."

Their mother, Johanna, now joined them. Her daughters showed her the section of the paper, but she didn't attempt to read it because her life still was lived only in the Norwegian language. Around home that was the only language used. Helmina explained the write-up to her mother.

"I don't think it is proper that they listed all the gifts," Johanna remarked.

"Why, Mother?" Helmina asked. "They do that for all the weddings now."

"It is like you are trying to show off," her mother explained. "It just isn't proper."

Helmina had also been reprimanded by her mother last Sunday after she had sat beside her new husband on the men's side of the church, instead of sitting with the women and children.

Now Helmina took time to re-read the write-up herself. Yes, it had been a great day for her and Nordlie. They had received many lovely gifts, and the money gifts would help them buy furniture when they moved into a place of their own. The day after the wedding they had gone to Canton to the photographer's to have their wedding pictures taken in their wedding clothes.

The May days passed quickly. When it got to be the last week of that month, Johanna had Johnny and Nordlie carry the big trunk down from the upstairs storeroom, and Ole and Johanna began to pack for their three-month stay in Norway. Besides the clothes for themselves and Henry, there was dress material and other gifts for the relatives they would be visiting.

On a trip into Canton, Ole Overseth subscribed for extra copies of the *Dakota Farmers Leader* to be sent to Norway when he was there. He wanted to keep up with the news while he was away. In the May 22nd issue of the paper it had been announced that the Hudson and Eden Townships would present the name of his brother, Pete Overseth, to the Republican County convention and ask for his nomination as representative to the South Dakota Legislature. Ole Overseth didn't want to be left in the dark about that turn of events.

On the afternoon of May 20th, the older members of the Overseth family attended the Mattie Rossum — Gunder Schiager wedding, and on June 6th, Ole and Johanna Overseth and Henry, together with Mr. and Mrs. Ole Rossum and Emma boarded the train at Hudson for the beginning of their Norway trip. Jens Bjorlie, the Moe community musician, also was on the train. He had sold his violin and was returning to his homeland.

Johanna hugged eight-year-old Jim and ten-year-old Tony, the sons she was leaving behind, and sternly instructed them one more time, *"Now you be good boys and mind Helmina and Nordlie."*

Helmina put her arms around her two brothers and assured her mother they would be fine. Johanna tried to be strong so she wouldn't lose control as she took Henry's hand and climbed aboard the train. Three months would be a long time to be away from her boys.

The rest of the Overseth relatives got in their buggies and headed for home. Now the newlyweds, Nordlie and Helmina, would be in charge of the Overseth household and of the farming operations for the next three months.

The morning air was sweet with the fragrant scent of new mown hay. Ole Nordlie drew in several deep breaths as he began mowing the last strip of hay in the field across from the Overseth house.

Yah, the women can have their perfumes, he thought to himself, as he luxuriated in the scents and scenes of the hayfield. I'll take the smell of new-mown hay any day.

The farming tasks were being completed on schedule. Nordlie had experienced a feeling of satisfaction after they finished haying on the Hudson farm and he looked over the large, well-shaped haystacks. Now they had come to the last hay field, the one across from the homestead, and it would soon lay flat, ready for the rake and the pitch forks to form it into more stacks. Then it was time to get on to other tasks.

Everyone in the family had been cooperating. John, Martin and Tony had been so dependable — up early every morning to help with the milking and other chores. Even eight-year-old Jim was there at milking time to put grain in for the milk cows and to feed the calves. And Uncle Christian was faithful with the wood supply.

As Nordlie reached the end of the field, the horses began to whinny and turn their heads towards the road. Ole looked and saw the most beautiful matched team of gray horses trotting down the road. Their heads were held erect and they trotted along, picking up their slender legs in synchronized movement. As they came closer, Nordlie recognized Rev. Hauge's buggy and waved. So this was the preacher's new team! Nordlie admired them as they passed by. Really, he thought, horses are the most beautiful animals God created, and he was anxious for the day he could purchase a team of his own.

"Hemmy," Martin called from the kitchen door, "what should I do with all this milk?"

Helmina wiped her floury hands on her apron and hurried to the door. It was the middle of the forenoon on the 22nd of June. Only an hour earlier Martin had left for the Moe Creamery and now he was back. Helmina was puzzled at his question and asked, "What are you talking about, Martin?"

"The creamery is shut down. Something is broken. They are sending all the milk back again. It may be two weeks before they get repairs for the pump," he explained.

"You had better go and tell Nordlie," Helmina advised. "Better go right away because the milk will sour quickly in this weather."

Martin turned to go, then hollered back, "The pigs won't mind sour milk."

When he gave Nordlie the details of the predicament, Nordlie shook his head and mumbled in a low voice, "Humph, now we'll be doing all that milking for nothing, but we mustn't waste it. We'll just have to feed the pigs some more . . . and the calves. Maybe Helmina could use more in the house. She could make some cheese. We'll hang another can down in the well to be chilled. Milk is good for us all."

Yah, Nordlie thought to himself, farming doesn't always go smoothly. You just have to deal with each problem as it comes up.

The summer days quickly passed, and then it was harvest and the click of the binder could be heard from early morning to late at night. The first of August brought hot weather for the hauling and stacking of the bundles, besides the other daily chores on the farm. It had been more than once during the past week that Ole Nordlie had wished for the pleasant cooler summer weather of Hurdal.

One day Nordlie came to the house very upset. He had been working with the hogs in the hot temperatures. His shirt was soaking wet with sweat, and his trousers were covered with mud and pig dirt. At the kitchen door he was met by his bride, Helmina. He shared with her his concern, "I think the pigs are sick. Some of them don't want to eat—or even move." He had come to the house with the idea that a cup of coffee and some sugar lumps would make things look brighter.

But Helmina handed him a basin of water and some soap.

"That hog odor on your clothes is fiercely nauseating, Nordlie. Here, go and wash up outside and I'll get you a towel and some clean clothes. You men folks can't sit at the table like this," she informed him.

At the supper table, the first thing that Nordlie announced was, "The pigs are sick." He and Johnny spent the whole supper hour discussing this distressing situation.

"It looks like the same thing the Rises had last fall," Johnny observed.

"*Oh nei, Oh nei, I hope not,*" Nordlie said.

Knud Rise, the Overseth's closest neighbor to the west, had the previous fall contacted hog cholera into his swine herd when he purchased breeding stock that was infected. Very quickly each and every one of his pigs died.

"Maybe it is just the hot weather," Helmina suggested. "Even people lose their appetites when it is so warm."

The next day two pigs were dead, and from then on it was a job each day to bury the dead ones. Nordlie felt bad because he had wanted everything to go well while the Overseths were away.

Chapter XI

Ole Nordlie directed the horses up to the Moe Creamery and began unloading the milk cans from the wagon. Several of the neighbors were unloading milk also. Everyone was talking about the hog cholera epidemic that was sweeping through Norway Township. He learned that the epidemic hadn't seemed to miss anyone. Knud Ekle, the father of one of the proprietors of the Moe Store, had his hog herd wiped out by the cholera. Everyone agreed that it wasn't fun to farm when things turned out like that.

Helmina had given her husband a list of groceries she needed, so Nordlie moved his team over to the store and tied them to the long metal hitching post that ran the length of the Moe Store. Claus Hegness, who was now the new clerk at the store, filled Ole's grocery order, and carried it out to the wagon.

Nordlie picked up his mail and turned to leave, but proprietor, Oluf Ekle, followed him to the door. Outside he spoke to him.

"Nordlie, now that you are married, I know you will be looking for a farm. I just wanted to let you know my folks are going to sell their farm . . . *in case you are interested.*"

Ole Nordlie's pulse speeded up. Of course he was interested!

"If you are, perhaps you should go see Pa," he added.

Nordlie shook his hand and said, "Thanks for telling me, Oluf."

The Knud Ekles lived just a quarter of a mile west of the Moe corner. It was part of their field the Lands congregation had purchased for the Lands church and cemetery. Yes, Nordlie was interested. He had watched the crops each year as they grew in Knud Ekle's fields. It was good land, a little rolling, with a creek running through it south of the buildings.

Yes, Nordlie was very interested. Then he stopped to speculate as to what price they would be asking for it. He would drive over there right away and find out. He was sure there would be others interested when the news got out.

Nordlie trotted the team up the Knud Ekle lane. A grove had been planted north of the buildings. There was a good house on the place, but nothing very much in the line of barns — only some make-shift sheds.

Knud Ekle was working in the yard as Ole got down from his wagon and approached him. Knud was a man of around 60 years. He had been one of the early homesteaders in the community, and the years of hard work and struggles showed in his stooped back and slight limp.

"Knud," Nordlie addressed him, "Oluf told me you are thinking of selling your farm. Is it true?"

Knud looked at him and slowly and determinedly nodded his head.

"That's right. I have found a smaller farm down by Fairview with mostly pastureland where I can raise a few cattle. I am through with pigs!"

Ole knew he still had the most important question to be answered. He cleared his throat and then inquired, "Tell me, what are you asking for this farm then?"

Ole wondered if Knud could hear his heart pounding as he waited for an answer.

"Well, Helene and I figured if the buyer would take over the $3000 mortgage, and give us $1700 cash, we could pay for the farm down by Fairview and be out of debt. When a person gets older, it is good to be free of debt."

"This is a big decision for us, Knud," Nordlie explained. "I'll have to think it over and talk to the Missus about it."

As he climbed up in the wagon, he added, "Don't sell it without giving me a chance."

"By the way," Knud added, "last year's taxes haven't been paid. Things have been kind of tight since Oluf bought the store. I'll tell you what I'll do, Nordlie," and then he laughed. "If you buy it and pay the taxes, I'll guarantee you'll never get hog cholera here." Knud Ekle chuckled some more.

Nordlie hurried home to the Overseths and had to speak privately with Helmina right away. He carried the groceries into the kitchen where she was making dinner. Tony and Jim were there, so he pulled her outside where they could stand and talk on the porch.

"Helmina, how would you like to buy a farm?"

There was excitement in his voice as he presented the proposition.

Helmina studied him, trying to figure out what he was talking about. Now she could see the excitement in his eyes.

"The Knud Ekle farm is for sale," he informed her.

"By the Lands church?" she asked.

He nodded his head.

This was indeed an exciting piece of news. After it had soaked in, she asked, "Do we have money to buy it? We can live at the Hudson farm, you know."

Nordlie smiled and answered, "Yes, I think we can handle it, providing the man who holds the mortgage will let us take it over."

As he stood facing her, he grabbed both of her hands in his and squeezed them several times.

"I have saved up enough money for the cash payment and I should be getting a money payment from brother Laurits for my share of *Nordlien* any day now."

He squeezed her hands again. *"Just think, Helmina, if we could have a farm of our own!"*

She smiled at him and nodded her head.

Ole Nordlie hoped this was not all too good to be true. Well, tomorrow he would drive to Canton to find out if it would be possible for him to take over the mortgage. And he must find out how much the back taxes were. A person can't wait around when there is something he wants!

Ole brought home good news. The mortgage could be transferred. For several nights he sat with paper and pen, adding and subtracting figures. He had to be sure he could handle this. If he had a farm, he would need to purchase machinery, horses and several cows. And they also needed some furniture. At times his head ached from figuring and from weighing the situation's pros and cons. Then there was the pressure of making a quick decision before the farm was sold to someone else.

According to the known expenses, Ole could see his way clear, but what about the risks involved? Perhaps he would have a bad year with no crops and no money to make the mortgage payment, or perhaps crop and livestock prices would fall. Then there was always the possibility of unforeseen costs and bills.

Helmina watched him as he wrestled with the decision. She knew how much he wanted that farm.

One morning both Helmina and Nordlie arose early, before the rest of the household had awakened. They were sitting in the kitchen having a cup of coffee while they discussed the situation. Then Helmina had a suggestion, "Nordlie, maybe you should go down to Hudson and talk it over with Uncle Pete. He would give you good advice. Besides, he would loan us money if we needed it."

Nordlie studied his bride. He knew she was just trying to help him, but he was a married man now and he would have to make decisions by himself. He couldn't run all over the country asking for advice. He was rather glad her father wasn't home; otherwise her father would probably have gone ahead and bought the farm for them, and he would still be only a hired man. Ole wanted to do this by himself. Besides, who could ever know for sure what the future would hold? No, it was he who would have to decide one way or another, and then they would have to live with the consequences.

"Helmina, if we should take this big step, it will mean that to start with we won't have much. Are you willing to get along without some things for a while?"

Ole knew Helmina had come from a home where anything that was needed could be purchased. Would she be dissatisfied when she had to do without?

"Ole, you don't have to worry about me. I can cook, sew and make do. It will be cozy to have our own home, no matter how simple it is. Anyway, we must not forget we will be in God's care, and just do our best and leave the rest to Him."

Ole Nordlie took a sugar lump and dipped it in his coffee. He sat for a few moments and savored the sweet coffee flavor as he thought about what his wife had said. How easy it was to get caught up in worrying about things that might never happen . . . instead of day by day trusting the Lord.

As he thought of things in that perspective, the whole situation began to look different. He laid his hand over Helmina's and looked into her eyes.

"Thanks for reminding me, Helmina."

She poured more hot coffee into his cup. He filled his saucer and sat and slowly sipped it. Now sounds were coming from upstairs, and soon Johnny and the rest of the family would be down. But now he had made up his mind.

"You know, Helmina, if we are frugal and only purchase what is absolutely necessary, I think we can get started on our own farm. Perhaps we should go over to Knud Ekle's today. We haven't seen the inside of the house yet. We should check it out before we buy."

She nodded her head.

They both smiled as they arose to get on with the duties of the day.

Chapter XII

"Come on in to the parlor," Ole Overseth invited. Everyone was hungry and anxious to eat dinner.

"It will be a little while before the women get the food on the table."

It was September 6, 1896, and Martin Overseth's Confirmation Day. It had been a long service at church. The guests, Uncles Pete and Hans Overseth from Hudson, and the Grevlos family, found chairs in the parlor. Klara Grevlos went to the kitchen to help her sister Johanna and niece, Helmina. Her son, Paul, had also been one of the confirmands.

Ole and Johanna Overseth and Henry had returned from their Norway trip only several days earlier, and they had much to share with their relatives. Helmina had done most of the preparations for the confirmation day.

"Well, how does it feel to be back home again?" Pete Overseth asked his brother.

"We were having such a fine time, I could have stayed longer. But then I was getting anxious about everything here at home too."

"How were our brothers then? How are they getting along?"

"They send greetings to both you and Hans."

Ole Overseth pulled up a chair and sat down. He had much to tell about his trip.

"Brother Johannes has gotten himself a magnificent farm in Østre Toten. *Buruld* is like a king's estate with enormous houses and barns. Yah, I guess he made a good choice when he went back to Norway, if you compare the little place he had here."

Ole Overseth fingered his beard as he thought about this. Then he went on, "Brother Johan, who lives on *Overseth*, is doing all right too."

Ole Grevlos spoke up. "How is everything in Vestre Toten then? Did you get to see all the Narums?"

"Johanna has some pictures that were taken at a big gathering there. The Ole Rossums came over and are on the picture too."

Now Ole Overseth in his loud direct way addressed his brother Peter. "Tell me, Pete, how does it feel to be *a politician?*"

Ole Overseth was proud of his brother and added, "You'll do all right, Pete. Everyone in this end of the county knows you after all the years they have been trading in your store in Hudson."

"Yes, now I have to go campaigning in the northern and western parts of Lincoln County. The November election will be here before I know it."

"Well, Pete, I'll say this: I am glad you are running for state representative. You will represent us well . . . and you know how to handle money. That's something they need some lessons on in Pierre."

Pete then turned to Ole Nordlie who had been sitting and listening. "Nordlie, what is this I hear about you buying a farm while Ole and Johanna were away?"

"It's being finalized, Peter. I think we'll be able to move into the house later this fall, when the Ekles get their corn picked."

"I must commend you, Nordlie. You made a wise purchase."

Ole Overseth joined in. "Yah, Nordlie, I've got to hand it to you. I don't think you could have found better land. And to top it off, it's close to us so we'll still see a lot of you and Helmina."

A voice came from the dining room. "Come and eat!" Johanna called. "Martin and Paul, you sit in the places of honor today."

There was much conversation around the table — so many questions about the relatives in Norway and so much to tell about the three months they spent there. Then the topic would switch to politics, with the South Dakota problems Pete was supposed to fix when he got to the Legislature. Of course they had to discuss the national election, which was causing a lot of attention in Lincoln County with Wm. Jennings Bryan running against McKinley.

Martin and Paul had to remain and listen to all the discussion. The younger children had left the table to go out and play. Finally Pete Overseth stood up.

"I've been sitting too long. I must get up and walk around a little after that big meal." He went over and put his hand on Martin's shoulder.

"Say, Martin, how are you coming on your cornet since you began lessons from Indseth?"

There was a special comradeship between Martin and his uncle.

"Why don't you show us how well you have mastered your instrument?"

Martin looked around to see if people really wanted to hear him. His father joined in, "Yah, Martin, get your cornet and give us a little concert."

When Martin came back with his cornet, his mother suggested, "Why don't you play some hymns, Martin? It's your confirmation day today, you know."

After he had played several hymns, Martin asked his Uncle Pete if he had heard Ole Bull's new song, "*Seterjenten's Sondag*." Professor Indseth loves this tune and plays it often on his violin when we have band practice. It sounds best with the violin, but I'll do it for you on my cornet."

Martin began the melancholy melody, which expressed the loneliness the dairymaid feels up on the *seter* on a Sunday morning. Ole Nordlie had never heard this song before, and the beautiful, sad tones hit home. It was as if it was his heart that was crying out this minor, lonesome tune. It had a real Norwegian flavor, akin to Edvaard Grieg's music. There was something about this song that made him lonesome for Norway.

Really, it puzzled Nordlie as to why he had these feelings because everything should be wonderful now. He had a new bride and would soon have a fine farm, but still his heart sang out in these lonely strains. He arose and said, "I think I'll go out and see if the cattle have water."

Johanna then announced afternoon coffee was ready. "Now, Papa, I think because this is a special day for Martin and Paul, you should have a prayer before we eat."

"Yes, it is a special day," Ole Overseth agreed. He bowed his head and began, "Our Father in heaven, today we ask your special blessing on Martin and Paul. May they always remember this day and the promises they made today. Thank you for your loving care that follows us all over the world, and thank you for the home you have given us and for family bonds. *Mange tusen takk* (Many thousand thanks). Amen."

It was October 8, 1896, and W. J. Bryan, one of the candidates for President, was campaigning in Dakota. He had left Sioux City, Iowa, that morning in the rain, had made stops in Elk Point and Hawarden, and after leaving Hudson, he made a stop in Canton where a big crowd had waited two hours to see the young Abe Lincoln of the West. He spoke for five minutes and shook hands with a number of people before his train rolled on to Sioux Falls.

Ole Overseth, his son John, and son-in-law, Ole Nordlie, had gone to Hudson to catch a glimpse of Bryan there.

Helmina Nordlie had spent the afternoon sewing kitchen curtains. She now began to gather up the material that had been spread over the kitchen table. She wanted to get things straightened up before her Mother returned from Ladies Aid.

Helmina held up the valances she had edged with crocheting. It would look nice, she decided. Now all she had left to do was sew a heading for the rods and she could hang them. A house seemed so bare without curtains. She wanted them ready when she and Nordlie moved into their own home next month.

As she finished folding the curtains and clearing off the table, her husband appeared at the back door and called, "Come outside, Helmina, and see your new horse."

Helmina grabbed her shawl, slung it over her shoulders and joined her husband. There standing tied to a post by the barn was a beautiful white mare.

"Where did you get her?" Helmina inquired.

"I ran into Erik Rise in Hudson today. He is back from out west with a number of the horses he has been raising there. He wanted us to stop across the way at his brother's farm because he had just the horse for you. You know we will be needing a buggy horse and one we can ride horseback on."

"Is she gentle?"

"Well, I led her home behind the wagon, but Erik guaranteed her and she does seem to be a fine animal."

"What's her name?"

"They call her Bessy."

Ole Nordlie walked around and inspected the horse. He looked at its teeth and at its hooves, and then slapped its flanks.

"See here, she has branding marks. She's a western horse, all right."

Helmina put her hand up to pet the horse's nose and was glad to see the horse was not nervous or skiddish.

Ole was happy. It looked like the horse and his wife would get along well.

"She's a pretty animal," Helmina said. "I've always wanted a white horse."

"We'll keep her around a few days and see how you and Bessy get along with the buggy. Erik has two other horses that would make a good team of workhorses for me. I'm going back tomorrow and look at them again."

Ole walked back to the wagon and showed Helmina the lumber, nails and other materials he had purchased in Hudson.

"Selmer Rise can begin fixing the upstairs of our home next week. I've got the supplies now. I saw Ovald Ekle today and he said his folks

were already moving out, and they wouldn't mind if Selmer began working on the upstairs."

The newlyweds walked together back to the house.

"I'm pleased with the horse, Ole. Now tell me, what about Bryan?
Did you and Dad get to shake hands with the next President?"

"It was a big disappointment. The Hudson depot was crowded with
people waiting to see him, but the train just slowed down as it went by
and Wm. Jennings Bryan came out to the rear platform and acknowledged
the cheers of the people by bowing and saluting. They explained he was
behind schedule, so he didn't have time to stop at Hudson."

"Well, you saw him anyway," Helmina remarked.

The presidential campaign was the topic of conversation everywhere
in Lincoln County, with Bryan and his Free Silver Party running against
McKinley. But politics wasn't the only topic at the Overseth home. Nordlie
and Helmina were getting ready to move, and they had many arrangements
to make.

When the Overseths had returned from Norway the first of
September, Ole and Helmina Nordlie had already made final arrangements
to buy Knud Ekle's farm. That fall Nordlie would still be helping with
the corn picking at the Overseths after they moved. But now he had to
buy a milk cow, a team of horses, some machinery, and some furniture.

Nordlie had hired a carpenter, Selmer Rise, to finish the upstairs
of their house and divide it into bedrooms and plaster the walls. They
were anxious to get this done before cold weather came.

Fall went by in the usual fashion with the trees changing colors and
finally standing bare. The first part of November, Helmina and Ole
Nordlie moved on their own farm right west of the Lands church.

Helmina lived close to her family, so the two and a half miles path
between the two homes was travelled almost every day, either by some
member of her family, or by Ole or her.

Politics had entered the Overseth family in a big way because of Uncle
Pete's campaign. The first of November, Peter A. Overseth won the election as state representative from Lincoln County, and would go to Pierre
in January for the legislative session.

Ole put in long days as he conscientiously worked with his farm and
livestock.

After living over a year in their own home, Helmina and Ole Nordlie
were blessed with a son. On December 16, 1897, Ingeborg Hanson came
over to deliver the baby boy. She was the midwife who had brought

Helmina into the world twenty-one years earlier. In her lifetime, Ingeborg delivered over four hundred little ones.

The Overseths were thrilled with the new baby that made them Grandpa and Grandma. The baby had another Grandma also, and Ole Nordlie wrote to give his mother this news.

> "*Kjaere Mor,*
> A big event has happened here in South Dakota. Helmina and I have a healthy baby boy for which we give God thanks. We haven't named him yet, but I wanted you to know as soon as possible. I'll write later and tell you his name. We are very proud of him.
> All three of us send greetings for a *Glade Jul* and a *Godt Nyttaar* (Merry Christmas and Happy New Year), dear '*Bestemor*' " (Grandmother).
>
> Love,
Ole

After things calmed down, and Christmas and the baptism were over, Nordlie one afternoon got out the pen and ink and paper to write a letter to his sister Ingeborg and brother-in-law Otto Rognlien. The baby was sleeping and Helmina also was resting. Ole wanted to give his family back in Norway more information about his little family.

Moe, S. Dakota
13 Feb. 1898

Dear Brother-in-law and family,
I received your letter awhile ago, and I hereby send you my hearty thanks. I see by your letter everything is well with you all, your health and otherwise. I can tell you the same is true with us. We have been healthy every day. Our little son, who now is two months old, is very happy, and good and is now growing to be big and fat. When I wrote to Mother about our little child, I couldn't tell her his name yet, as he had not yet been baptized, and we had not decided for sure about the name up to that time. But now I can tell it to you, and will you please tell mother his name is Obed Joel.
I see by your letter you are now involved in politics and many other activities. I, on my part, am so busy, and can't find time to take part and follow along in that respect. I am a Republican, and I am a subscriber to a large Republican newspaper, the "*Skandinaven,*" a Chicago publication. I can tell you about politics in America, but it will take too long, and my letter will be too heavy if I try to explain it all. I presume you read in your newspaper how politics are going over here.

I see by your letter I am finally to get some money from Norway. I haven't had any word regarding that yet. I presume that Th. (Thorkel) Langseter, the treasurer at the Hurdal Savings Bank, has forgotten to mail it to me. It also came as a surprise to me that brother Ludvig is engaged to be married. He had been saying he was going to emigrate to America, but evidently didn't mean to at all.

So I will close my letter for this time with the heartiest wishes to you all from

Ole Nordlie and Family

Please greet those at home at Nordlien from us. O.N.

Chapter XIII

Helmina Nordlie cleared the dinner dishes from the kitchen table. It was haying time and today she had fed four extra men. Her little eighteen-month-old son, Obed, had been put down for his nap. Now the kettle was boiling, which meant the water was hot so she could wash the dishes.

Helmina put her dishpan on the table and was about to fill it, when she heard the screen door slam. At the kitchen door stood her husband with a little boy in his arms.

"Helmina," he said, "look who I found coming up our driveway."

Helmina immediately recognized the little lad as the pastor's four-year-old son, Siegfred Hauge.

The Hauge family was the Nordlie's nearest neighbor, just living a half mile to the east.

Siegfred looked at Helmina with his merry little eyes and smiled.

"Siegfred wants to know if he can have some cookies," Ole explained.

He set the little fellow down on a chair, and Helmina began to question him, "Tell me, Siegfred, where is your mama?"

"Home," he answered. "She's feeding the baby."

"Where is your papa then?" Helmina wanted to know.

"Town," he responded.

"Oh my, oh my, he has come by himself! I think he has *run away*. I'm sure Emma is searching all over the parsonage for him."

"Can I have a cookie?" Siegfred had not forgotten what he had come into the house for.

"What shall we do, Ole? Would you have time to take him home? I just got Obed to sleep. It would be difficult for me."

Helmina shook her head and added, "Emma must be just sick!"

Helmina went to the cookie tin and got several cookies for the child.

"Yah, we'd better get him home as soon as possible," Ole agreed. "I'll have the rest of the men hitch up the horses and go ahead to the hayfield. I'll follow as soon as I get back."

Ole bent down and explained to the little boy, "Siegfred, you eat your cookie and I will get Bessy out and you can ride horseback with me home to your mama."

The little boy wasn't worried. He had decided to go visiting, and that is what he did.

When Ole came, Helmina lifted Siegfred up on the horse; then she hurried back into the house and watched as the white horse trotted by the window, with her husband holding tightly to little Siegfred, who was seated in front of him. They were headed down the driveway toward Moe.

When Ole got Siegfred home to his frantic mother, she explained that several times before, they had discovered the lad walking down the road and had taken him home. This day in June, 1899, was not the last visit he made to the Nordlies by himself.

The first Sunday in August, 1899, Ole and Helmina Nordlie walked to church, as was their custom when services were at Lands. Ole carried Obed because his little legs couldn't keep up with their pace. Besides, he might fall and get the beautiful clothes Helmina had sewn for him dirty. That morning when Helmina was dressing Obed, Nordlie had remarked, "With all those ruffles, people will think we have a little girl." But Helmina had informed him that that was the style for little boys now. She liked to be up-to-date.

Today Pastor Hauge was preaching on II Timothy 2:19. He read the verse slowly and emphatically.

"The Lord knoweth them that are His."

Pastor Hauge pointed to the altar painting of Jesus hanging on the cross, and said, "I want to ask you, are you building your life on *Him*?"

After a pause, he continued, "Someone besides you knows the answer to that question. It is awesome to realize that Someone knows every thought you think, every desire you have, every word you speak, and He knows if you belong to Him. He can read your heart. May your heart be saying, '*Yes, Lord*'."

When he finished the sermon, he closed the large Bible on the pulpit, adjusted his glasses, and cleared his throat.

"I have an announcement to make today. I have lived in your midst for nine years now, and it is with some sadness I must tell you that I am resigning. Today was my farewell sermon. I feel my life being directed in a different area. I have enrolled in medical school in Sioux City, Iowa, and classes begin soon."

This came as a big surprise to everyone. It had been good to finally have a pastor living right in the community. Pastor Hauge had done much to better things. His fine stately altar stood as proof of that, and many remembered his visits at their homes with President Tuve, as the men tried to collect money so Augustana College in Canton, South Dakota, could go forward.

But Rev. Hauge had been a strict pastor, and some people were glad he was moving on, especially the young people he had surprised after a wedding reception Pastor and his wife had attended. When the Pastor decided to come back later in the evening, he found the young people dancing in the barn, which he informed them he was not happy about.

On August 11, 1899, Pastor L. J. and Emma Hauge and sons, Siegfred and Phillip, loaded up their possessions and left the Moe parsonage to take on another life work.

Ole and Helmina Nordlie felt sad because they had enjoyed having the Hauges for neighbors. It was Rev. Hauge who had baptized Obed. Johanna Overseth was especially sad because she had taken Mrs. Hauge under her wing, and the Hauges had chosen her as godmother of their youngest son, ten-month-old Phillip.

Sunday, March 3, 1901, was a cold winter day. When Ole Nordlie came in from doing the chores, he stood by the round pot-bellied stove in the dining room and warmed up his hands and feet.

The hired girl, Ragnhild, had made breakfast. She was a newcomer girl from Norway who had been working at the Nordlies since before Christmas. She was very good with Obed, who was three years now.

Helmina came into the kitchen while the rest of the family ate breakfast.

"Aren't you feeling well today, Helmina?" her husband asked.

"I think I'll just have a cup of coffee," she said.

Ole looked at his wife with concern, for it was almost time for their second child to be born.

Helmina rubbed her back with her hand.

"I have a feeling it will be today we will need the midwife."

After breakfast, Ole went outside and curried Bessy and put the harness on her. It would be wise to be ready in case he had to make a trip to get the midwife today.

It was 9:30 a.m. when Ole came into the house again. He was met at the door by the hired girl, who nervously told him she thought he should get the midwife. When Ole went in the bedroom to Helmina, she agreed, "I think it's time you went for Mrs. Storkson."

Ingeborg Hanson, who had delivered Obed, had retired from her mid-wifery duties, and now Ole and Helmina had contacted a Mrs. Storkson, who lived almost three miles west of them, to come when it was time.

Ole Nordlie quickly changed his clothes and put on his big fur coat. He looked at the clock in the kitchen. It was ten o'clock. He didn't want to worry his wife, but he remembered that today services were being held in Romsdal Church, located west of them, where the Storksons were members. He must hurry before Mrs. Storkson went to church. After hitching Bessy to the sleigh, he threw in the big fur lap robe because he didn't want Mrs. Storkson to freeze.

Ole headed west a little over two miles and just before he got to the Romsdal church, he turned north, up a long driveway. Everything was quiet when he came on the Storkson farm. He knocked on the door, but there was no answer. Some of the Storkson horses neighed at Bessy, and this brought the hired man out of the barn.

"Is Mrs. Storkson home?" Ole asked.

He was getting anxious because time was not to be wasted today.

"They went to church," the hired man informed him.

Ole quickly climbed back in the sleigh and slapped Bessy with the reins. It was almost time for the church services to begin.

Outside of the Romsdal Church many horses, buggies and sleighs stood. Ole tied Bessy to a hitching post and ran up the steps into the church. He paused in the doorway and looked over the congregation. Everyone was standing and singing the first hymn. Ole glanced around to see where the Storksons were. By the time he had discovered them, Mrs. Storkson had seen him. She whispered to her husband, picked up her bag, and joined Ole. They hurried to the sleigh, made a quick stop at her house, and were home on the Nordlie farm in less than an hour.

Mrs. Storkson immediately went into the house while Ole unharnessed the horse. He felt relieved that Helmina now had dependable help.

Later that afternoon, a baby girl was born to Ole and Helmina Nordlie.

"You have a beautiful baby daughter, Nordlie," Mrs. Storkson informed him, "and your wife is fine, but tired."

After Mrs. Storkson had washed the baby and put on the gown Helmina had sewn and decorated with embroidery, she bundled the little girl in a blanket and showed her to Ole.

Ole went into the bedroom to see his wife. "A daughter was just what you wanted, wasn't it, Helmina?"

Helmina smiled, "I'm just happy the baby is all right."

Ole held Helmina's hand.

"Now you can sew fancy clothes. Now you have a little doll to love and dress."

Ole was proud of his little family. Yes, now he would have to write to Norway and tell his mother about their sweet little daughter. He thought to himself how nice it would be if they could call the baby '*Marte*' after his mother.

On March 31, 1901, *Thelma Louise Marie Nordlie* was baptized in the Lands church. Helmina had felt they should give their daughter an American name. Rev. Strass, the interim pastor, performed the sacrament. Her sponsors were her Uncle John Overseth and his wife, Rena (Jacobson); their neighbor, Charley Ekle; and her aunt, Anna Overseth.

In 1900, Pastor Strass had written in the Lands Church records, "*The congregation's second church, whose cornerstone was laid in 1879, has for several years been in a dilapidated condition and on certain occasions been too small. The question being asked is whether the congregation should repair the old church and build an addition to it, or whether a new church should be built.*"

Many meetings had been held at Lands church during 1900 and the winter of 1901. Finally it was decided to build a new structure. Plans had been chosen for an eight-sided building. In March of 1901, the bid of a contractor from Hawarden, Iowa, had been accepted. To begin with, the thought had been that material from the old church would also be used in the construction. The men discussed how and when they should begin dismantling it. The contractor's bid had included $400 worth of material from the old church.

At one of these meetings Ole Overseth had remarked,

"It is too bad to tear the church apart. If it could be moved, it would make a good building for someone to use."

Nordlie needed some buildings. He had been trying to repair the little sheds he had, and the idea of a good building for his horses and cows appealed to him. He had been dreaming of building a large, big barn, but he didn't have the money for that. This building he could get for the sum of $400.00. But how would he move it the half mile to his farm? He would have to look into that first.

Later that evening, Ole Nordlie shared his plan with his wife.

"Use a church for a barn? Would that be right?" she asked.

"Would it be any better to tear it apart?" he inquired.

A thought came to Ole, and he passed it on to his wife. "You know, a stable was the first place Jesus dwelt when he came to this earth. I don't think He'd mind."

"Yes, that's true, Ole. I didn't think of that."

Ole contacted the men in charge of the building and purchased the old church for $400. He began making plans on how he would move it to his farm. That spring when they were ready to begin construction, the church was jacked up, and wooden skids were slid under it. A large block and tackle was used, and with Ole's eight horses, the building was moved the half mile across the field and set on a foundation south of the Nordlie house. Ole then had the big job of remodelling the forty-five by thirty foot building so it could hold his eight horses and the milk cows, calves and colts.

There was something special about having a building upon his farm that had been used in the Lord's service. He had good feelings about it as he went in and out of it everyday.

And every day Ole and Helmina Nordlie could look across their field and see the tall steeple of the magnificent new eight-sided Lands church, and the sounds of the church bells were often heard.

Chapter XIV

Helmina sat in the rocking chair in the dining room feeding her little daughter, Thelma. It was the middle of the morning, and the September sun was shining in through the east windows and making designs on the wooden floor.

"Mama," three-year-old Obed called as he came running in from the kitchen. "Mama, can I go outside and see the kittens?"

Helmina put her finger to her lips and spoke softly. "You must be still, Obed."

She shushed him again and added, "It is time for your sister to take her nap. Why don't you stand by the window and look outside? See if you can see Papa working in the field." Ole Nordlie was plowing the field where he had recently harvested his 1901 oats crop.

Obed picked up some of his blocks and dumped them on the window seat, then crawled up on the window seat and studied the outdoor activities while intermittedly building his blocks.

Suddenly in a loud voice he called, "Mama! Mama! Here comes a wagon."

The baby lying in Helmina's arms jumped, but soon closed her eyes again.

"Mama, it's *Bestefar* (Grandpa)."

Helmina brought baby Thelma into the bedroom and laid her in her cradle.

Obed turned on his stomach and gradually lowered himself to the floor, then took off like a whirlwind to the kitchen door. Helmina followed him and opened the door. There was her father, Ole Overseth, tying his team to the hitching post. She let Obed run out to meet him. *Bestefar* picked up Obed and in his loud manner called, "Hemmy, have you got the coffee pot on?"

"Of course, come on in, Father," Helmina invited.

"I've been over at the Moe Store and suddenly I got lonesome for my grandchildren."

Ole Overseth carried Obed into the house. He sat down on a chair by the kitchen table with Obed's little arms still clinging to his neck.

"Well, my big boy, are you happy to see *Bestefar*?"

"Yes, *Bestefar*, I was watching in the window and then you came." He gave his grandpa a hug.

Helmina got her big white cups and the saucers down from the cupboard and poured coffee. She sliced several pieces of bread and put the butter and sugar, sugar lumps and *gjeitost* (goat cheese) on the table. Her father buttered a slice for Obed and sprinkled sugar on it, then fixed a slice for himself with goat cheese.

"You'll never believe the news over at Moe Store today. I tell you it isn't good, that's for sure!"

He paused while he took a sip of his hot coffee.

"Someone from Canton came out to the store today and reported that President McKinley had been shot yesterday. *The President of the United States*! Everyone feels so sad and upset about it. It doesn't sound like he'll make it."

Helmina gasped at the news.

"Why, he's hardly been in office six months. Why would someone want to shoot him?"

Helmina remembered reading about Lincoln's assassination . . . but that was fifty years ago and she had thought people were more civilized now.

"How awful," was all she could say.

"Yah, it is awful alright. What is this country coming to? It had been a vigorous campaign last fall with Wm. J. Bryan running for the third time and losing to the McKinley—Theo. Roosevelt ticket, but I don't think that had anything to do with it. It must have been someone who wasn't in his right mind."

Her father took another drink of his coffee and then let Obed dip a sugar lump into it.

"We think the world should get better and better, and then we hear a thing like this."

He decided to have a sugar lump himself.

"Well, I'll tell you, it was almost as great a shock a couple of weeks ago to have a robbery at the Moe Store, right here in our Christian community."

"Have they caught the thieves yet?"

"No, today they still didn't know any more. $400 worth of shoes and dress goods is a lot of merchandise to lose. I'm sure the proprietors, Claus Hegness and Knute Jacobson, aren't too happy about it. That would be their profit."

"I can't see that anyone would be brave enough to break in when the owners were sleeping upstairs," Helmina said, "and the new clerk, Ed Linde, was sleeping over the blacksmith shop."

"It's funny they didn't run off with some of the new John Deere machinery, or wagons or buggies because these were all setting outside."

"I hope they find the thieves soon."

After taking several bites of his sandwich, Ole Overseth added, "When I was at Moe today, I watched the carpenters working on the new public hall they are building over there. Knute Jacobson and Claus Hegness will make Moe into a little town. You just wait and see."

Her father then changed the subject. "Well, how is the little one?"

"I just put her down for her nap."

"I can hardly believe she is already six months old. How fast time goes."

Ole Overseth wasn't one to sit long in one place. He let Obed down on the floor and arose. "I must go in and peek at my little granddaughter before I leave. I'll be very quiet."

"By the way, Hemmy, many of the men from church have been suggesting that we should ask Nordlie to be our new 'klokker.' You might mention it to him so he can have an answer ready when they approach him. He'd do a fine job."

After a busy fall, Christmas arrived and with it the Christmas letters from Norway that Ole Christian Nordlie always waited for. Christmas Eve was especially happy in 1901 with two little ones to make the holiday a special time for both the Nordlies and the Overseths. And then it was time for Ole Nordlie to sit down and answer his Norway Christmas mail to keep contact with his family over there.

A smoky haze filled the kitchen as Ole Nordlie came in for his morning coffee. Helmina had just finished frying doughnuts. She was piling the cooled ones into the big crock. After laying a plate over the top, she carried the crock into the pantry and set it on the floor.

It was a cold March day in 1902. The sun was shining but a north breeze made a person aware it was still winter.

Ole sat down at the kitchen table as his wife poured coffee. She set a plate of fresh doughnuts and a bowl of sugar lumps in front of him and left to check on her baby daughter.

Baby Thelma was still sleeping, but as she walked through the dining room she noticed Obed sitting in a corner. Helmina stopped to see what he was doing. He had been very quiet all morning. As she approached him, she noticed he was picking at his nose, and rubbing it.

"What are you doing, Obed?" she asked.

He turned his head away from her.

"Is something the matter, Obed?"

At first he didn't respond, but then he rubbed his nose again and gave the direct answer as only a four-year-old would.

"Something's in my nose, Mama."

Helmina bent down. "Here, let me see."

That wasn't a good position so she set Obed on a chair.

"Where is it that it hurts, Obed?"

He pointed to the left side of his nose. There up in his left nostril she could see a dried green pea.

"How did you get this in your nose?"

"It was on the floor last night and I was playing with it."

"And you put it in your nose?"

Obed looked down at the floor and didn't answer.

Helmina wondered what she should do to get it out. Her fingers were too big to get at it. It would only push it farther in. She called to Ole.

"Come here and look at Obed."

Ole left his coffee cup and was soon at Obed's side. Helmina explained the situation. Ole carried Obed to the bay window where it was lighter and examined his son's nose.

"Blow your nose, Obed," his father instructed.

Obed tried and tried, but the pea didn't seem to move at all.

"We've got to do something, Ole," Helmina said. "Maybe I could get one of my crochet hooks. Maybe we could get that around it to pull it out."

"It looks like the pea has already begun to swell. I really don't think that would work. It may only push it farther up. *Nei*, we'd better not try working in his nose any more. It could get lodged up higher."

"We have to do something," Helmina stated. She was getting more nervous and upset every minute.

"Well," Ole finally said, "maybe I'd better take him into Canton to the doctor. The doctor can take care of this. That would be the safest."

Helmina began to relax a little as she considered this possibility.

Ole continued, "I have several errands to do in Canton anyway. But we'll have to get going as soon as possible. I'll have to take the wagon."

"Can you manage alone? It's a pretty cold day to take the baby out."

Helmina and Ole were just beginning to discover all the unexpected worries that went with being parents. Helmina bundled Obed up and wrapped a scarf around his face so only his eyes were peeking out. Ole climbed on the wagon seat, put Obed in his lap, folded the fur robe around them both, and headed out on the hour and a half drive to Canton.

All during the day as Helmina cared for little Thelma and did her housework, her mind was on her son and her husband. Oh, she hoped the procedure would be done without much pain . . . or scaring Obed. She chided herself for letting the dried peas fall to the floor last night when she had taken them out to soak for the soup they were to have for supper tonight.

It was just getting dark as she heard a horse's whinny and the lumbering noise of the wagon coming up the driveway. Helmina went to the kitchen door to meet them. Nordlie carried Obed to the door and set him down, then went back out to get the new addition to their household — *a little black pug house dog.*

Nordlie explained it this way to his wife, "When I got to the doctor's office, Obed was so scared and I felt so sorry for him. I remembered that Pastor Hauge had left his dog in town and they were looking for a home for it. To cheer Obed, I promised him if he was a big boy, we'd see if we could get a dog to take home with us. You know how he's begged for one. And it worked. He was so brave. Well, that is the story. Now we have a house dog, and his name is Carlo. By the way, where is the dog?"

Both Ole and Helmina looked around. Obed had gone to sleep on the dining room floor, but the dog was not there. Helmina went into the kitchen. Then she heard a crash. It came from the pantry. *And there was the dog!* It had pushed the plate off the crock and was helping itself to doughnuts. Helmina's fresh doughnuts!"

"Get out of here, Carlo!" she screamed.

Ole had heard the commotion, and he was soon in the kitchen too. It was kind of funny but he didn't dare to smile, even a little bit. All he said was, "I guess we won't be having doughnuts tonight."

"But the pigs will," Helmina disgustingly added.

She didn't know if she was going to like having a dog in the house. She knew she would have to begin doing things differently.

Obed and Carlo turned out to be the best of friends. And it kept Obed occupied so Helmina could get her daily tasks accomplished.

And the dog became a fat spoiled pet.

Graduation picture of Anna Overseth—June 5, 1902.

Chapter XV

The one-horse buggy drawn by the beautiful white mare headed for the Overseth home. Helmina Nordlie was holding the reins, and her other arm was tightly clasped around her little daughter sitting in her lap. Beside her on the seat was her four-and-a-half year old son, Obed. Helmina was making a visit to her parental home. Although she lived only two and a half miles away she didn't come often by herself for it was difficult to watch the two little ones and do the driving also.

It was a nice May day in 1902. As the buggy travelled up the Overseth lane, Helmina took in all the familiar sights — the white fence around the house — the house where she had spent all but the last five years of her life, the apple trees which were now in bloom, and the arbor covered with grape vines. Yes, she had a special feeling for this place.

Helmina turned to her little son. "We're almost at *Bestefar's*. It won't be long now."

"I'll look and maybe I can see him, Mama."

Helmina's thoughts again returned to all the old familiar things. There were the hens with their little chicks all pecking at the earth, looking for worms to eat. This farm held all of her childhood memories. She wondered if this was the way her husband still felt about Nordlien, his old home in Hurdal. Often she had sensed his fierce loyalty to Norway. Now they had their own farm home, but perhaps old memories and the feeling of belonging to their childhood homes would never go away.

Today was the seventeenth of May — *Syttende Mai*! For her husband and father and mother, this day always held a special meaning. Especially this year. She had to admit it didn't excite her that much. They all had been talking for weeks about Professor Indseth's family concert which was to be held tonight at the Moe Town Hall in observance of the Norwegian Independence Day.

As the buggy entered the Overseth farmyard, Helmina's father came to meet them. He had been planting seeds in his flower bed by the back door. After tying Bessy to the hitching post, he lifted Obed down from the buggy and set him on the ground. Helmina then handed her father her fourteen-month old daughter and alighted from the buggy herself.

"Anna has been waiting for you," her father informed her. Sister Anna was home for the weekend from Augustana College in Canton.

"I think the women are busy sewing."

He gave baby Thelma back to Helmina and took Obed by the hand.

"Obed, why don't you stay outside and help me in my garden? We men have to get our work done, don't we?"

Helmina let herself into the house. There standing in the dining room was her sister. Today the dressmaker was fitting her graduation dress. It was a floor-length gown of white organdy with two rows of organdy ruffles around the bottom of the skirt. The dressmaker was down on her knees on the floor measuring for the hem.

Helmina's eyes took in all the delicate details of the dress. A wide ruffle went over each shoulder and came together in the front in a "V" at the waist. The three-quarter length sleeves had been decorated with narrow tucks, which ended in a wide ruffle hanging below each elbow. The yoke also had decorative tucking, and the high neckline was edged with a narrow ruffle.

"Oh, Anna, I like it," Helmina assured her sister.

"It's almost finished," the dressmaker informed them. "I just have to take it in a little at the waist and sew up the hem."

"It's really beautiful, Anna."

Johanna stood beside them watching, her hands on her hips, nodding in agreement. *"Saa fine. Saa fine."*

"I'll wear the large cameo pin Pa bought me for Christmas. It will fit right here in the middle of the yoke." Anna pointed to the spot.

"That will be lovely," Helmina agreed.

"Well, I'd better take off this dress so Maggie can finish it." Anna went into the downstairs bedroom to change.

Helmina set little Thelma down on the floor and she was soon toddling around. Grandma Johanna put out her arms to her granddaughter, but when the little girl realized she was loose from her mother, she wanted to take off and investigate everything in the room.

"Where's Obed?" Johanna had just discovered he wasn't with Helmina.

"He's outside with Pa."

"Yah, Pa decided to work around the house this afternoon so he could get an early start with the chores. He and the boys plan to take in the *Syttende Mai* concert. Are you going, Helmina?"

"I hadn't really planned to. It's too difficult to take the children along. Nordlie talked of going, though."

"Oh, you should go, Helmina. Why don't you leave the children here? Anna will be home with me. She has to work on her graduation speech, but the children won't bother her. They'll be asleep as soon as it gets dark. Yah, just leave them here, Helmina. It isn't good that you always must stay home."

"I am planning on attending Anna's graduation, though. I've already asked one of the Grevlos girls to come and stay with the children that day. Ole feels he can't be away all day because he's trying to get his work done so he can be gone the week of the church convention in Minneapolis . . . since they felt the '*klokker*' should be the delegate."

"Yah, you certainly must go to Anna's special day, Helmina. You can ride with us. But you should go tonight too. Pa says it will be an outstanding program with the talented Indseth family putting on the concert. You love good music, Helmina. Just leave the children here now, and you can stop by for them after the concert."

"There's one thing, Mother. I didn't bring along many clothes for Thelma."

"Oh, that's no problem. We'll manage alright. Just go and enjoy yourself."

"If you're sure, Mother."

"Yes, but you'd better go home and get ready. Pa says if a person wants a seat tonight, he should get to the Moe Town Hall early."

Helmina and Nordlie hurried with supper and chores. Nordlie had been planting corn, but he quit at coffee-time because celebrating the *Syttende Mai* was very important to him. There had only been a few years any observances had been held. Although they arrived very early, the hall was already almost full.

Nordlie found a seat for Helmina and went outside to stand with some other men by one of the open windows. People kept coming, and soon there were as many people outside as inside.

The hall was a long, narrow building with many windows along each side. Benches ran across the room and were divided by an aisle, and the stage was at one end.

About fifteen minutes before eight o'clock, the Indseth family members began tuning their instruments. Professor Andrew K. Indseth and his wife Inger had come to the United States from Norway in 1889, along with their four children. Five more children had been born here in South Dakota. As a young man in Norway, Andrew Indseth had been trained as an organist, had studied voice, and become proficient in both violin and cornet. There wasn't an instrument he couldn't play. After coming to America, he had been giving individual lessons on instruments and voice, and directed many choirs and bands, both in Lincoln and Minnehaha Counties. He had taken over the Normanna choir at Moe after Jens Bjorlie went back to Norway, and he was also directing the Moe Band boys.

Professor Indseth's sons all had musical talents and the Syttende Mai concert included special solos and duets, along with the family orchestra. Inger Indseth and several of the daughters had beautiful voices and this gave variety to the program. To celebrate the day, Professor Indseth tried to include many Norwegian numbers.

About half way through the program, Professor Indseth announced a composition by the Norwegian violinist, Ole Bull, entitled *"Seterjenten's Sondag."* He placed his violin beneath his bewhiskered chin and drew the bow across the strings. If there was only one instrument he could play, it would be his violin. Indseth's wife sang along as he performed this number. Her rich coloratura soprano voice brought out the sad tones of the melody:

"I gaze on the sun as it mounts in the sky,
It soon will be time for Gudstjeneste (church services).
I wish I were home to follow along
As folks wend their way to the kirke (church).

Ole Nordlie was standing by the open window. The wistful sound of the violin music again touched his emotions, and the words of the song directed his thoughts back to home. In the darkness he could imagine Snultra, the *Nordlien seter,* and feel the young *budeia's* lonesomeness on a Sunday morning.

I know it is time for the church bells
To ring in the valley
And be resounded again
As echoes join the pealing from the steeple."

Standing there in the dark, Ole Nordlie closed his eyes. Again he heard the sounds of the church bells from the Hurdal church as they rang out and then as each sound was multiplied by the echoes. It wasn't that way here in flat South Dakota. When the bells rang out from the Lands church on the corner, the sound spread out and disappeared. Often he had caught himself listening for the echoes.

Nordlie didn't pay much attention to the rest of the program. Here in the dark he had time to think of home and the mountains. It was the mountains that made the echoes. It was the mountains that gave Hurdal its rugged beauty.

After the concert was over, Nordlie and Helmina picked up their sleeping children and went home. When Nordlie had unharnessed the team and come to bed, Helmina was already asleep. He lay there in the dark. Tonight the blood in his veins was pure Norwegian. He had had a chance to celebrate the *Syttende Mai* with others from the Fatherland. The Norwegian melodies had awakened again his lonesomeness for Hurdal. In his mind's eye he could see Nordli Kampen mountain, its sides covered with beautiful green fir and white birch, and the other mountain that arose across from it, forming the Hurdal valley. And he thought of his childhood home. And the day he left for America. He could still see his mother standing wiping her eyes with her apron, and his sisters who now were grown. Why, Ingeborg now had a family of her own, and Ludvig was married too. And he thought of Mother, who was there waiting for him to return so she could see him again. He had told her many times he would. How happy she would be to look at him once again, and his wife and little family. He decided he would just have to start saving for the trip home. He'd have to make it a priority. Tonight his evening prayers there in the dark concluded with this verse from Psalm 121 which he had memorized for his confirmation many years ago:

"I will lift up mine eyes unto the mountains
From whence cometh my help.
My help cometh from the Lord
who made heaven and earth."

It was a comfort to know God would be his helper, no matter on what terrain he was living. Perhaps it was just a matter of looking up.

The Overseth surrey pulled up outside the Nordlie house before eight o'clock on Thursday morning, June 5, 1902. Ole, Johanna, Jim and Henry, all dressed in their best clothes, had stopped to pick up Helmina. Today Anna would be graduating from college. The one and a half hour trip should bring them to the Augustana Lutheran church on Third Street in the western part of Canton in plenty of time for the 10 a.m. commencement exercises.

They were very glad they had an early start because the church wasn't very large, and when they arrived it was already getting crowded. However, they all did find seats.

The church had been decorated for this special occasion with flowers and plants. The seats for the ten graduates were draped in their class colors of cerise and nile green. Over the arch hung the class motto, NOT FINISHED BUT BEGUN.

When Palma Anderson began playing the prelude, the class marched up to their seats near the platform. The four young ladies were dressed in white, with corsages of fresh flowers pinned to their left shoulders. Ole and Johanna Overseth, and Helmina, all looked with pride at Anna as she stood by her chair in the front of the church. Today her thick brown hair lay in soft waves around her face, in a bouffant fashion, and where it was done up in the back, a small spray of lilacs was tucked in. Those who knew her could tell Anna was a little nervous. Who wouldn't be if one had to give a long speech before this packed church?

The ten graduates each had to present an oration on some topic. Anna's was entitled "*Determination vs. Genius.*" In it she argued that genius is determination, or rather the result of determination. She emphasized the greatness of determined action and patient labor. At first her voice was weak and a bit shaky, but then she cleared her throat and as though she was acting on her own words, with determined effort she spoke out, "There is no success dependent on luck or chance . . . but it is determined effort that leads to success."

Ole Overseth agreed with every word she spoke. Her voice carried even to those people in the corners in the back. He was glad to hear her attitudes on life. He wouldn't have to worry about her future.

Each of the graduates took his or her turn. Hans M. Dale of Howard, South Dakota, spoke on "*Civilization.*" He compared and contrasted occidental and oriental civilizations — the western civilization meeting the eastern. Now the West looks back upon the home whence it started and upon a civilization bound down and fettered by tradition. Mr. Dale closed with a strong plea to America to deliver China from the chains of tradition with which she was bound.

Overseth listened with special interest to Dale's speech because Anna had been dating him.

Each student in turn presented his or her thoughts on some subject. Ole Overseth was thankful for the monies he had given to keep Augustana

College going. Today he was hearing what Christian education does for young men and women.

The college choir and a male quartet each presented several selections, and President A. G. Tuve in a few well-chosen words called the class's attention to the life before them, then presented the diplomas to each member.

Afterwards, the excitement of the graduates and their families and friends was given expression as everyone congratulated and visited with the honored ten.

It was announced that President and Mrs. Tuve would give a reception in the evening for the graduates, students, alumni and families, but Ole and Johanna decided to leave Anna at school and return home. Ole directed his team downtown and tied them outside the Farmers State Bank. He had to stop and say hello to his brother Pete, who had moved to Canton and now was the president of this new bank. Pete came out and greeted everyone.

"Have you driven by to see all the new construction in town?" Pete asked. "You must take a look at how Canton is progressing. Let me show you all the activity."

Ole moved over and Uncle Pete took the reins. They made a tour past the new luxury hotel that was being built by Judge Rudolph, and Pete pointed out all the other new store buildings coming up in that area. Then they headed south so he could show Johanna, Henry, Jim and Helmina the new Chautauqua facilities. The large round auditorium was to hold 1500 people. Ole had seen it before when he had been along with the Old Settlers committee as they made plans for their annual picnic to be held there later in the month. This would be the second year of the Chautauqua, but this year the grounds were more complete. And there on the river, tied to the dock, was the new Sioux Queen river boat.

Uncle Pete didn't have time to take them to see the new Augustana College Main building that was being constructed, or the building going on east of town where the Indian Asylum facilities were being built, but he described it all to them.

"What do you think of our progressive little town now?" Pete asked. They were all impressed and told him so. But Ole added, "Those of us out on the land are getting modern too. On the way to town this morning, we noticed men setting up telephone poles. They plan to have telephone service to Moe in a couple of months.

"And another thing, Pete, by September we will have a mailman who will deliver our mail right to our driveway. I never thought I'd ever see such progress in my lifetime."

Then it was time for Ole and Johanna and their family to head home.

The graduates had many more activities scheduled. In the afternoon the students and alumni would take a ride on the new Sioux Queen down the Sioux River. Anna, together with Martin and Tony, who also attended Augustana, would return the next day after all the activities had ended.

Chapter XVI

Helmina awoke to the sounds of thunder. Gusty winds were rattling the windows. Not until she reached her arm to the other side of the bed to awaken Ole, did she remember his side was empty. Her husband had been gone now for one week, attending the 1902 church convention in Minneapolis. But today was June 24th and he would be coming home.

Helmina climbed out of bed, threw a shawl over her long nightgown and went to the bedroom window. As she watched, the sky lit up in blinding flashes and then all became pitch dark again. The thunder continued to roll and rumble, with intermittent loud claps, and the wind seemed at times to make the house tremble. Helmina went into the dining room where the bay window gave her a better view. There, during the lightning flashes, she could see the strong winds bending the trees.

This was not an ordinary thunderstorm. Helmina became nervous and decided she should awaken Martin. Her brother had been staying with her and the children, and doing the chores while Nordlie was away.

Oh, if Nordlie were here, he would know what to do, she told herself. She was lighting the kerosene lamp when Martin joined her.

"Hemmy, I think we'd better get to the cellar. That wind sounds bad."

Martin had slipped on his pants and his boots. He was buttoning his shirt as he spoke.

"I'll run upstairs and get Obed, and then we'd better hurry down to the cellar."

Helmina went into her bedroom and picked up little Thelma. She quickly wrapped a blanket around her, then grabbed a quilt from the bed to take with her to the cellar.

Martin was soon back with Obed in his arms. The little boy, only half awake, kept repeating, "What's the matter, Mama? What's the matter?"

They all headed for the kitchen door. Now they would have to go outside and down several steps before they got to the outside cellar doors.

Martin set Obed down. "I'll go and open the cellar doors and then come back and get Obed," he said. Helmina and the children stood in the kitchen and watched. When the lightning flashed, she could see Martin struggling against the wind to get the doors open. Then Martin, with Obed in his arms, and Helmina, carrying baby Thelma, hurried out into the flashing windy night, the blanket ends flapping, and raced for the open cellar doors, and down into the safety of the cellar. Martin reached up and finally got the doors closed above them.

Helmina lit the short candles she kept in the cellar, which she used to find her jars of fruit when she came down for supplies. Then she spread the quilt on the floor and placed the children on it, all the time sending up prayers asking for God's protection. Helmina had always been fearful of tornadoes.

Baby Thelma and Obed were both wide awake now. Helmina wished Ole was there. Only once had they headed for the cellar, and that time they had come up to find only rain and no other damage. She hoped that would be true now also.

From time to time Martin went to the cellar doors to hear if the wind was still blowing. After about an hour he reported it was raining, and water was leaking down through the cellar doors. They waited a while longer, and then he lifted the one side to see if it was safe to come out. The rain was still coming down, but more gently, and the wind had let up.

Martin and Helmina, with Obed and Thelma, made a dash for the back door. The house was still there. Helmina lit the lamp again and checked the downstairs. When she came into the bedroom, it was a mess. One of the windows had been broken and the rain and debris had blown into the room.

"Martin, you'll have to go to the shanty and find something to cover this window because the rain is still coming in," Helmina instructed. She picked up the wet rugs and took the bedding off the bed. She got rags and began mopping up the floor, trying to be careful of pieces of glass. She closed the door because she didn't want the children in there. It was beginning to get light now.

"*Helmina! Helmina!*" Martin shouted. He opened the bedroom door and excitedly informed her, "*I think the barn has been hit! It still isn't light enough to see, but there is an awful moaning and neighing coming from there. Some of the animals must be hurt!*"

Martin was soaking wet from his trip outside, but he had found some pieces of lumber and a hammer and some nails. He quickly covered the window so the rain couldn't get in. Helmina opened the back door, and they both could clearly hear the animals.

"What do you suppose has happened?" Helmina asked her brother.

"The horses were tied in the barn last night. That's all I know. It's getting lighter now and the rain has just about stopped, so I'd better go out and check."

With the dawn, Martin and Helmina could see what the wind had done. The roof of the barn which Nordlie had remodelled from the old Lands church had been partially blown off, and it looked as though several other buildings outside had been damaged, and many trees seemed to have been uprooted.

When Helmina saw this destruction, her heart was filled with thankfulness to God for the protection He provided her and her little family.

Martin and Helmina went out to investigate and discovered a portion of the roof had landed on the backs of the horses that were still standing in their stalls. The horses seemed to be scared and neighed in noisy confusion.

"We'd better not go in there," Martin warned. "The whole roof may collapse."

Helmina worried about her white mare. *"Bessy, Bessy,"* she shouted. She tried to use calming words. *"Bessy! Are you alright?* Nice Bessy."

A loud whinny answered her, and put her mind at rest. What would she do without Bessy?"

"What are we going to do?" Helmina asked. "Some of the animals may be badly hurt."

Martin walked around the barn, trying to check things out and see what shape the building was in. He returned to the north side of the barn again and reported to his sister. "I think it is only the south side of the barn roof that has been damaged. But the corner that was torn loose landed on the horses, and it is too big for you and I to get off by ourselves. The milk cows are alright though. It's a good thing I let them out last night. Now they're standing by the west barn door, waiting to be milked."

Just then their father, Ole Overseth, rode up on his horse.

"I'm relieved to see you folks are alright." He looked around and then asked, *"But where are the children?"*

"They're fine; they went back to sleep. But you should see the mess in our downstairs bedroom! A window was broken and the rain and leaves and dirt came in."

"I was worried about you folks over here. That was a bad storm. There are uprooted trees all over. I saw debris scattered all along the way.

Even the fine steeple on our new church is lying in pieces on the church lawn.

Another session of neighing began.

"What are we going to do about the horses?" Helmina asked. "Part of the roof has fallen on them, Pa. Bessy is under there too. From all the noise, I think most of them must be alive, but they may be hurt."

Ole Overseth was ready to get into action. "Get the saw and the ladder and we'll see what we can do."

Helmina went to the house to check on the children and continue her bedroom clean-up. Ole and Martin sawed off portions of the loose roof section, then pulled the remainder to the ground, relieving the horses' backs from their unwanted burden. After inspecting the horses, they found none of them had been badly hurt. Bessy had a large tear on her rear right flank where nails had gouged her. Several of the horses limped as they were loosened from their stalls.

Ole Nordlie came home later that afternoon to a farm that needed much repair and clean-up, but his family was safe and that was the most important thing.

This tornado of June 24th, 1902, had done an enormous amount of damage, for it had covered the whole area from Canton and south to Hudson, over twenty-five miles. Two churches in the community, the Augustana Synod Trinity church, and the Hauge Synod Romsdal church, both had been leveled and the beautiful steeple from the new Lands church had been blown down, and the building weakened.

Every farm had uprooted trees and other damages, but in the whole area only one person had been killed. This was a woman east of the Moe community who had come back up from the cellar to get some milk for her baby when she was hit by flying debris.

The lumber yards were busy all summer and fall, loading lumber and other supplies for all the farmers who had repairs to make. And Ole Nordlie had to find a hired man to help him with the farm work so he could assist the carpenter in getting his buildings usable again. He was very fortunate that the brother of Ed Linde, now the new proprietor at Moe Store, had arrived in America. Reinert Linde was a hard worker and very dependable and fit in very well. He was more like one of the family than a hired man.

It was a busy summer and fall and Ole Nordlie didn't get his usual Christmas letters written to Norway, only a short greeting to his mother, but after Christmas it was time for Ole Nordlie to sit down and answer his Norway Christmas mail:

Moe, S. Dak.
Jan. 25, 1903

Dear Brother-in-law and family!

I suppose you are waiting for an answer to your letter to me. I had hoped to answer it right after Christmas, but it has been postponed until now. Today I will send you a few words. First, I want to tell you we are all healthy and living quite well. We have had no snow this winter until yesterday when we had a snowfall of about 3 inches. I see by the newspapers you in Norway had plenty of snow during Christmas.

Now I want to congratulate you on your new farm. It was very wisely done of you, Otto, because in Hurdalen there was no real future for folks of the middle class, and even less for the ordinary working class. I also see you are now a resident of the real good farming area in Toten.

During Christmas, I had a visit from a man from Christiania who knows you well. I was not too well acquainted in Toten, but I have gotten good information about Eastern Toten from him. This spring he will be going back to Norway, and then you will receive a visit from him. He promised to visit all my brothers and sisters.

Last summer I was busy rebuilding several of the buildings on my farm, so I have had much work with that besides the farm work. I have only had one hired man, and it is different here than in Norway. The women do not care for the cows and cattle. I have 40 cattle, 8 horses and 65 hogs. Our main product is to raise corn and hogs. The corn is fed to the hogs. This year I am doing well with both corn crop and the hogs, as the selling price is now twice what it was before.

My farm is in a good locality, a large Norwegian settlement. Our church is located on my farm and now they are talking about a railroad that might be built about a five minute ride from here, where a town may be started. This would be convenient for us, as now it takes me a one-and-a-half hour drive to the nearest town.

My desire to return to Norway is more and more becoming a driving longing as the years pass by, and I go and think about it and long for the day I can go. My wife is very anxious to make a trip over there to see Norway, and she asked me today if we could go this spring. But I don't see how I can get away this spring. Possibly it could happen, but I can't quite see it now. So I must close for now. You and all of your family are heartily greeted from me and my family.

Your Brother-in-law
Ole Nordlie

P.S. Greet Mother from me, and my brothers and families, and Mathilda. I send hearty greetings.

98

Daughter Thelma Nordlie — Circa 1904.

Chapter XVII

After the tornado of 1902, the new eight-sided church at Moe was a busy place. The Lands congregation offered to share their facilities with the two neighboring churches until new structures could be rebuilt. Often services were held both Sunday morning and afternoon, and sometimes during the week.

In March of 1903, a new pastor, Rev. Simon J. Nummedal, arrived at the Moe parsonage. He was not a stranger to the Moe families, for he had been a dedicated member of the Board of Augustana College at Canton for several years.

When Nummedal arrived at Moe with his belongings, he did not own a cow and he had to obtain milk for his family from the neighbors. It was just a quarter of a mile to the Nordlie farm and every day he or a member of his family came with the pail to keep the Nummedal household supplied with this necessary foodstuff.

The first day Pastor Nummedal knocked on the Nordlie back door, Helmina ushered him into the kitchen.

"Come on in, Pastor," Helmina invited. "You must have a cup of coffee while Nordlie gets your milk."

Pastor Nummedal sat down at the kitchen table. Helmina busied herself, getting dishes and doughnuts on the table. Young Obed stood against the wall and looked the new pastor over. This man had a full beard, but kindness shone from his face.

"Come over here, son," Nummedal addressed Obed.

The boy cautiously stepped closer.

"What's your name, lad?" Nummedal was trying to get acquainted.

Slowly and softly came the reply, "O-bed Jo-el Nordlie."

"Tell me, do you go to school?"

"Not yet." Then he brightened as he offered this information. "But I can read and spell."

"How old are you?"

"I will be six when I have my birthday."

Now Obed grew bolder and asked the pastor a question.

"Do you have any boys?"

"You are looking for someone to play with, aren't you?"

Obed nodded his head.

"*Nei,* I am sorry to say I haven't. But I have lots of girls."

"How many?"

"Can you count?"

Obed nodded his head.

"See if you can count them on your fingers as I tell you their names."

Obed grasped the little finger on his left hand, ready to begin the exercise.

"There is Agnes, Lillie and Hannah and Laura and Sarah. That is five. Right?"

Obed nodded his head.

"Then there is Valborg, and Stella, and Esther, Opal and Elsie. How many did you count?"

"All my fingers got full." Obed counted his fingers again and asked, "Ten?"

"Correct! Did you say you could spell too?"

Obed nodded his head and smiled.

"Can you spell 'cat'?"

Obed quickly responded, "*K-A-T—kat.*"

"Good! You can spell in Norwegian. That's a fine big boy. Now can you spell your name?"

Quickly Obed answered, "*O-B-E-D---Obed.*"

"But tell me, can you spell MY name?"

Obed hesitated. "I don't know."

"Tell me, boy, can you spell '*Nummedal*'?"

Obed was very serious. As he thought it out, he looked up at the ceiling and down at the floor and finally he turned to the pastor and began, "*Num—N-U-M.*"

"Correct. Go on."

Obed rubbed his nose and took a deep breath. "*me—M-E.*" He took another very deep breath and added, "*dal—D, D, D.*" He then sounded out an "aa" and continued "A" and ended with "L". Now he went over the whole name again. "*Num—N-U-M---me—M-E---dal—D-A-L. Nummedal!*"

"Wonderful! You are some boy! Why, you do better at spelling my name than many big people."

When Nordlie came with the filled milk pail, Helmina poured up the coffee.

"Pastor," Nordlie asked, "how is the building project coming over at the parsonage?"

"When I left this morning, the carpenters were already hard at work. We'll soon have plenty of bedrooms for our family."

Shortly after the arrival of the Nummedal family, the congregation had voted to build a sixteen by twenty-eight foot addition to the parsonage. Besides the pastor and his wife and ten daughters, Tante Stromsness also lived with them.

"Nordlie, could I ask a favor of you? If you hear of a good milk cow or two that are for sale, would you let me know? When the grass gets green in the pasture, we can just as well have our own cows."

For several months Pastor Nummedal made daily visits to the Nordlie farm to keep his family supplied with milk. Obed was no longer bashful around him, but became a great friend of the pastor. And the Pastor was so impressed with the way Helmina had been teaching Obed to read and spell in Norwegian, that one day he brought along a book to give Obed — a *Lasebog* (Norwegian ABC reading book), which Obed studied diligently.

After that, the Nummedals always had two or three milk cows. When the grass was short in their little pasture, one of the girls or Tante Stromsness would herd the animals in the road ditches. Tante Stromsness always had her knitting with her. She made use of that time, because it took many pairs of mittens and sweaters to supply a family of ten children.

"The strawberries will be ready in time for your birthday, Helmina," Ole Overseth informed his daughter.

He had stopped by on a trip to the Moe Store.

"Will you be coming over to help me celebrate?" she asked.

Overseth had his granddaughter Thelma on his lap, and she was trying to dip a sugar lump into his coffee.

"*Passe deg*! (Be careful!) The coffee is hot, Thelma!"

After helping her, he took a sip of the hot coffee and set the cup back on the saucer.

Now he addressed his daughter, "Yah, Helmina, you can be sure of that! And I'll bring you a pailful of strawberries.

Helmina's birthday was June 14th, which in 1903 fell on Sunday.

"Why don't you and Mother and the boys come over? Nordlie won't be working and we can have a nice visit."

She thought a minute and added, "I think I'll invite Uncle Pete and Auntie Tetterud too. I've been thinking of having them out here for some time."

Ole Overseth's brother, Peter, now lived in Canton where he was president of the new bank. He was still a bachelor, but he had taken on a family responsibility. Ole and Peter Overseth's aunt, Margrethe Tetterud, lived alone in Canton. She had had a difficult life. Now even her daughter had married and moved away. Peter had taken his aunt under his wing. He had found a nice little house for her across from the East Side school, and every Sunday afternoon he went to visit her.

"I'll go over to the Moe Store tomorrow and ring Uncle Pete on the telephone," Helmina told her father. "It's already Tuesday and a letter would be too slow. I hope they can come."

"That sounds enjoyable. I'll bring plenty of strawberries."

After her father left, Helmina began making plans. She would make an angel food cake and serve the strawberries on top with whipped cream. Her hens were laying very well now, so she could spare the thirteen egg whites she needed for the cake. And then she would serve fresh bread with cheeses and some dried beef and cold roast. And she should bake some cookies. Yes, she would roll out some sugar cookies. Everyone liked them. And she hadn't made rosettes for a long time. She had plenty of lard on hand and they would look so festive.

And then another idea came to her. When we are having company anyway, maybe we should invite Pastor and Mrs. Nummedal too. She would talk to Nordlie about it when he came in for dinner. Yes, that would make a nice group.

Helmina had just gotten the Sunday dinner dishes put away when the Overseth surrey drove up the lane with her mother, father and younger brothers in it. Helmina had been busy the last few days getting ready for her party. Yesterday her father had brought her a pail of beautiful red strawberries from his patch and she now had them all washed and hulled, ready to be served over the angel food cake and whipped cream. She took off her apron and went to the front door to greet her parents.

"Ho, here is the birthday girl!" her father proclaimed in his usual loud manner. "Yah, I remember so well the day you were born."

"Happy Birthday, Helmina!" Johanna added.

As her parents stepped up on the porch, Obed came running and shouting, "Mama, the Nummedals are walking up the driveway." All of their guests were arriving at once.

Nordlie tied the Overseth team to the hitching post and he strode across the south lawn to the front porch.

Helmina ushered both her mother and Mrs. Nummedal into the parlor. She had opened the west windows and this afternoon a light breeze was blowing, making the lace curtains gently ripple.

"Well, Mrs. Nummedal," Johanna asked, "are you finally getting settled after all the remodelling and building over at the parsonage?"

"Oh, yes, everything is fine. Auntie Stromsness is there to help, so I've had time to get the girls all settled in their new bedrooms. They are so pleased with them."

"That's good."

It was quiet for a few minutes while the ladies settled into their chairs. Johanna straightened her long black skirt and smoothed it over her knees. Mrs. Nummedal sat down in the rocking chair, then with both her hands she patted down stray hairs that had blown out of place on the quarter mile walk to the Nordlies. Now with her foot she put the rocking chair into motion, just barely moving. She laid her head back against the rocker to relax after a busy Sunday. Suddenly a thought came to her. She stopped the rocking movement and sat erect.

"I'll have to tell you ladies about something that happened this morning. Do you remember last month at Ladies Aid when your neighbor, Enke Eckley, borrowed a common pin from me to use in the sewing she was doing that afternoon?"

They both remembered.

"Well, today, before services, she stopped at the parsonage and handed the pin back to me. I told her, '*Oh, nei, Mrs. Eckley, you return a pin?*" She insisted that I take it and added, "I shall not owe anyone anything."

Mrs. Nummedal shook her head and repeated, "It was just a common straight pin."

"I'm not surprised," Johanna remarked. "She is a dear woman. So honest and conscientious. She lost her husband many years ago when the children were all small, and it hasn't been easy for her. She knows the value of a pin."

Now the sound of buggy wheels came through the open window. Helmina arose. "I'd better go to the door and greet Auntie Tetterud."

Peter Overseth was driving a horse and buggy he had rented at the livery stable in Canton. He helped his aunt down from the buggy. She was a little whisp of a woman, dressed in a long black dress, with a little white crocheted collar around her neck. She carried her cloth bag on her arm. In her other hand was her hearing horn.

Nordlie met them. "Welcome. Did you have a good trip?"

Margrethe Tetterud put her hearing horn to her ear and pointed the large end at Nordlie, "What did you say?"

Nordlie repeated his question.

"Did you have a good trip?"

Peter quickly answered for them both. "This was a fine day for a ride."

Helmina ushered Auntie Tetterud into the house. Before she opened the door, Helmina called to her husband, "Nordlie, will you keep an eye on Thelma?"

Their daughter was two and a half years old now. Nordlie helped the little girl down the porch steps and she ran over to where Obed, Henry and Jim were sitting on the grass, trying to teach Carlo some new tricks.

"Would you men like to go inside too?" Nordlie invited.

"Oh, let's stay out here on the porch and enjoy the beautiful day," Uncle Pete suggested.

"Yah," Ole Overseth agreed. "This weather reminds me of summer in Norway.

Ole Nordlie went to get some chairs for them to sit on.

Pete commented, "When a person works inside everyday, this fresh air is a treat. I don't get enough of it. But I try. Early each morning another roomer at the hotel and I go for our daily constitutional. We walk one mile west of town and one mile south, then continue east and north again to the downtown. Four miles every day. And we get back in plenty of time so I can put on my necktie, have breakfast and get to work. When a person has a job inside, he has to find some form of exercise and get some fresh air.

"Well now, Pete," his brother chided him, "if you lived on the farm, you wouldn't have to worry about exercise. Isn't that right, Nordlie?"

Ole Nordlie nodded his head. He had now gotten all of the men seated on the porch.

Nummedal entered the conversation by addressing Nordlie. "We noticed you have telephone poles all the way up your driveway now. I was telling my wife it won't be long before the Nordlies will be talking to '*the Central Lady*'."

"This is a line that will continue west into Pleasant Township," Nordlie informed him. "We have all been helping to get the posts down. It will probably be another month before we get hooked up with Canton."

Ole Overseth cleared his throat. "I heard a funny account the other day about a farm couple from the Canton area who had gotten a telephone."

Here he stopped and chuckled.

"They were asked if they were enjoying their telephone and both the husband and wife nodded their heads and agreed. Then the woman said . . ."

Here Overseth chuckled some more and repeated his last few words, "the woman said, 'but now that it is spring we will have to go out and get the field work done and we won't have time to listen any more'."

All the men laughed.

Pete remarked, "It sounds like it was a social investment more than a business instrument."

Ole Overseth commented, "Well, now life won't be so lonesome for many families who don't get out much. That is good."

They all agreed.

Helmina had gone into the kitchen to get the lunch prepared. She was in the entry pumping water and filling the blue enamel coffee pot when Auntie Tetterud stood in the doorway. Her great-aunt had followed her into the kitchen and was offering to help. She stood there with her hearing horn in her hand. Helmina assured her she could get things done by herself, but her great-aunt lingered in the kitchen.

First, Auntie Tetterud walked to the window. She laid down her horn and felt the curtains and inspected the crocheted edging on them. Then she studied the picture Helmina had hanging on the wall. Next, she went to the spice cabinet. It was fastened to the wall and it had six compartments. She pulled out one drawer and looked inside. It was full of whole black peppers that Helmina would grind for the pepper shaker. She pulled out the next drawer, and there she discovered whole cardamom with the shells on. She continued opening all the drawers. Suddenly Helmina heard her great-aunt speak to her in a loud scolding voice,

"Oh, NEI-DA, Helmina!"

Helmina set the coffee pot full of water on the stove and came over to see what her aunt was talking about.

"Oh, Nei-da, Helmina. I didn't know you smoked tobacco!" Her aunt was shocked, and spoke the word *"tobacco"* with disgust.

Helmina looked at her aunt, who was holding a dark brown ginger root in her hand. Helmina tried to be patient and pleasant as she explained to her aunt, who was hard of hearing, that what she had in her hand was not tobacco but ginger root which she shaved off as a spice in her baking.

Finally, she encouraged her aunt to go and visit with the ladies. Auntie Tetterud reluctantly picked up her hearing horn and headed for the parlor and in a low monotone voice mumbled, *"Yah, etter det det er!"* (Yes, that's the way it is!), which was her favorite Norwegian old Toten expression.

When the coffee was ready, Helmina brought all the food into the dining room and invited her guests to the table. She had picked several irises that were in bloom and had them in a bouquet in the center of the table.

She seated the children in the kitchen.

When all the guests had found seats, Nordlie asked Pastor Nummedal to have the table prayer. The pastor bowed his head and began,

"Our dear Father in Heaven, we thank you for the lovely day you have given us. But most of all, we thank you for HEALTH so we can all be here today and have this fine fellowship with family and neighbors---and for HEALTH to enjoy this good food which has been set before us. You are so good. Amen."

Each person sitting around the table on thinking it over, wholeheartedly agreed and in their hearts added *"Amen."*

Good health had always been one of the blessings in Ole Overseth's life. He was always full of vim and vigor, interested in everything and willing to help whenever he could. The summer and fall of 1903 were full of community activities, such as the picnic in the Gubbrud grove located in the same section as the Overseth farm, to which hundreds of people turned out. There were short speeches by Pastors Nummedal and Thormodsgaard, and a number of selections by the Moe Band. But the most important part of the day was the offering taken for the Beloit Orphan's Home.

In October, the dedication of the new main building at Canton Augustana College was an occasion both the Nordlies and Overseths attended. But work did not come second-place on either farm and fall found the men picking corn and getting ready for winter.

On November 14th, Ole Nordlie made a trip to Hudson for supplies and stopped in at the Overseths on the way. When he returned home, he shared with Helmina his concern.

"I must phone to Canton for the doctor." Their phone had been hooked up for several months now, while the Overseths didn't have one as yet.

"Both your father and mother asked me to. Your father isn't getting over his chills and now he's running a fever. He's becoming impatient lying around the house and anxious to be well again."

Helmina too was concerned.

Papa has never been sick before. But it's good he'll see the doctor. Getting soaking wet last week when he was fixing the well was bad for him. And the weather that day was so cold too. You'd better ring the doctor right away, and perhaps he can get out here yet this evening."

But the doctor's visit didn't help. Ole Overseth began coughing and running a high fever. His family and his brother Pete and Pastor Nummedal visited him every day.

Several days later, Helmina came home very discouraged. As they were eating supper, the telephone rang — one long and two shorts. That was the Nordlie's ring, and Helmina hurried to answer it. It was her Uncle Pete.

"Hemmy, I think everyone will agree that we must try to do something for your father. It is so sad to see him worsening every day."

"Yes, if only there was something we could do," Helmina was quick to respond.

"I'll tell you what I did. When I returned to Canton on the train this afternoon, I got on the telephone and rang a specialist in Sioux City, a Dr. Warren. I also arranged for a special fast train to take the doctor from Sioux City to Hudson. He'll be coming to the Hudson depot tomorrow in the early evening, at 7:30. Do you think Nordlie could pick him up? or else get someone else to do it?

"Yes, Uncle Pete. We'll see that he gets to Pa's bedside as soon as possible."

"Martin and I will be coming out again tomorrow afternoon."

Since September, 1903, Martin Overseth had been working as a bookkeeper at the new Farmers State Bank, where his uncle was president.

"I hope this specialist can provide some help for your father," he added.

"*So do I, Uncle Pete. So do I.*"

The doctor arrived at the Overseth home Tuesday evening and stayed overnight, returning the next afternoon. Ole was now delirious part of the time. After watching over the sick man, the specialist reported, "There is nothing more that can be done. He has a severe case of pneumonia and it is very critical."

Saturday evening, November 21st, at 9 p.m., the fifty-seven-year old Ole Overseth succumbed to his illness. Around his bed stood his wife and seven children, his son-in-law and his two brothers, Peter and Hans.

Chapter XVIII

The Moe Store was a busy place on Saturday, December 11, 1903. Men and women were milling around. A number of people were looking for Christmas gifts. Several ladies were examining the bolts of material on the big table, trying to choose cloth for the sewing they were doing for Christmas. And supplies were being purchased for Christmas baking.

Barrels of fish, salt pork and molasses stood by the door, and the grocers had gotten the lutefisk shipment in.

Along the wall behind the long counter, rows and rows of canned goods set on shelves in orderly fashion. One of the proprietors, Knute Jacobson, was at the counter filling an order for Enke Eckley. She visited with him as she waited.

"Have you heard how poor Johanna Overseth is getting along?" she asked.

At the sound of the word *"Overseth,"* several other ladies and the two men standing by the pot-bellied stove came over to join in the conversation. The one man, August Johnson, volunteered an answer.

"Yah, poor Johanna. Now she is just taking one day at a time, trying to keep things normal for the family."

Enke Eckley broke in, "It will be a hard Christmas for her. I remember how it was that first Christmas, having '*his*' chair empty."

She brushed her rough hand over her cheek, and her lips quivered as she slowly shook her head from side to side.

The other man asked, "Yah, but what is she going to do? Maybe she will move to town. Say, Knute," he said, addressing the proprietor, "will Johnny be taking over the farm? He's the oldest. You ought to know since he's your brother-in-law."

Knute diplomatically and graciously told them he had heard nothing about it, but injected, "Overseth's family aren't the only ones who miss

Ole. Each time Ole came in the store, everyone brightened at his cheerfulness and friendliness. This community will miss him."

August cleared his throat and added, "Yah, he was like a brother to me. We homesteaded the same year. He was a neighbor who couldn't be beat."

The two ladies shook their heads.

"Nei-dah, it is so terribly sad."

The other added, "And such a shock! He was too young to die. Why, two of his boys haven't even been confirmed. They aren't even in long pants yet. *Poor Johanna!*"

An elderly man who had been listening joined the group and felt he had something to add. "Overseth's farming operation was so large with all his cattle, hogs and land, I tell you it will take a good manager to keep things going. Those boys at home can't do that."

August interrupted, "Oh, Nordlie has been coming over almost every day to see that there is feed for the livestock and that the necessary work gets done. And they still have the same hired man."

One of the ladies spoke up, "Perhaps Martin will give up his job at the Farmers State Bank and come home and farm."

August was anxious to answer her. "I don't know about that. Martin never really has cared about farming. He's been away at school a lot of the time and now he has that job at the bank. Sure, he's worked on the farm, but he's had no experience running a farm."

He paused a moment and then added, "Yah, and what about Martin and his music? He'll never give that up."

August cleared his throat again and finished his part of the conversation. "Oh, I guess Johanna is doing all she can do right now—just taking one day at the time. Maybe in a few months things will become more clear, and she'll know what to do."

All the people standing around him had sad expressions as they voiced their feelings.

"It is so sad."

"He was a good man."

"It sure is too bad."

Knute Jacobson packed Enke Eckley's groceries in her large basket. She tied the shawl over her head, put on her mittens, picked up the basket, and headed out the door to walk the mile west to her home.

Ole Nordlie had had a restless night. He had been turning and tossing for hours. He knew why. He had too much on his mind. Finally he got up and put on his clothes. In the dark early November morning, he went to the kitchen to start the fire in the cookstove. He would put the coffee pot on and pour himself a cup, then maybe in this early morning hour he could think things through.

Nordlie took some cobs and a few pieces of wood from the cob basket. After he got the fire going, he filled the coffee pot with water from the pail in the entry. A thin layer of ice was on it today. Nordlie dumped in some coffee, and then set his chair close to the stove and waited for the room to warm up while he let his busy thoughts ramble.

It had been a year now since Ole Overseth's passing. Yes, it was now November 21st again. It had been a hard year for everyone. How Overseth had been missed! Nordlie recalled the first upsetting months after his father-in-law's death. No one knew what to do. The leader had fallen and all concerned wondered how life would go on. At that point Johanna had been so indecisive. The shock of Ole's rather sudden passing, and missing him was not the whole pain. It was picking up the pieces and going on, trying to keep the Overseth farm as much like he had established it.

Then Nordlie's thoughts turned still farther back in time. This hadn't been the first time he had gone through this. After his own father's death, life had been upsetting too, but his home farm was a small-scale operation compared to Overseth's estate. And his mother, Marte, was well acquainted with the farming operation and could keep things going. On the other hand, Johanna Overseth knew very little about the Overseth business. She had been busy bringing up children and keeping the household running. Furthermore, she couldn't speak English, so she had left all business matters to her husband. Now she didn't know what to do. The farm must be kept in the family. She was definite about that. But who would take it over? John didn't want to move from the Hudson farm where he lived. Jim and Henry enjoyed farming but they were too young, just 14 and 15. Tony was still attending Augustana College, and Johanna knew how important it had been to her husband that his children have an education. Finally, in the spring, Martin had agreed to give up his job at the bank and move home to help out. But in the end, Nordlie had to be the overseer to see that things were going right. *Yah, Nordlie thought, the responsibility of two farms this past year has been too much.*

Many things had been left up in the air following Overseth's death. Ole did not have a will, so Johanna had petitioned to have Ole's brother, Peter Overseth, as the administrator of her husband's estate. And then there was the upsetting matter with Johnny. After building and fixing up the Hudson farm where he lived with his little family, and making some payments on it, he had only the oral agreement he had made with his father, and no written agreement or deed. Now both Johnny, and Ole Byhre, from Presho, were asking for deeds from the administrator. Byhre had borrowed money from Overseth to buy his ranch several years earlier. This was the ranch where Overseth sent his young cattle for grazing, later shipping them home for fattening. Byhre too had made payments but because he also had only an oral agreement, he had no deed or written agreement to show his ranch ownership. Yes, life had been upsetting for everyone this past year.

Recently Uncle Pete had had several talks with Nordlie about what should be done next. John didn't want to move. Martin finished getting the 1904 crops in and decided he didn't want to farm the rest of his life. Neither did Tony. Then there was Jim. He was the farmer in the family. Johanna wanted him to have a chance, but he should go to agricultural college at Brookings first. That was Uncle Pete's advice. In the meantime, someone must farm the Overseth land.

Uncle Pete had found a nice house for Johanna in Canton and he had been encouraging Nordlie to leave his own farm for a few years and rent the Overseth farm.

"You'll have the fine big barn and other good buildings. Everything is built up so you can raise a large number of cattle and hogs."

Pete had also talked to Johanna's sister, Klara Grevlos, and her husband, who were looking for a farm to rent and they could move on Nordlie's farm. He had it all set up.

"It will just be a matter of a couple of years until the younger boys can take over. It would really help Johanna out."

Now the smell of coffee filled the kitchen. Ole Nordlie got a cup and poured himself some. It was steaming hot, so he filled his saucer to give it a chance to cool. Then he sat and sipped from it.

The dish with sugar lumps was sitting on the table. That would be still better. Now with his coffee and sugar lumps he could really think. And this was what he must decide. Would he be willing to move to the Overseth farm and leave his own? This was not something he would decide without weighing the situation thoroughly. His wife, Helmina, thought this was a good idea and she was excited about moving back to her old home. It was no strange place to him either, for he had spent many years there too.

But Ole was a little disappointed. Helmina knew that for several years he had been planning a Norway trip. If he made this move, he would have to put that off. He was so anxious to introduce his mother to his wife and little family, and he would so love to see Hurdal again. Was he willing to let this dream be postponed? Nordlie dipped a sugar lump in his coffee and slowly savored it.

When it came right down to it, Nordlie almost felt locked into a *"yes"* decision. If he didn't go with the plan, what would they do? He took another sip of his coffee. Yah, he guessed he should quit resisting and agree to the plans. It might be, as Uncle Pete said, a good opportunity for him to get ahead. By raising more livestock in the well-built facilities he could realize more income. Maybe he could get enough money to build a nice big barn on his own farm. The year of 1904 would soon be ending, and Nordlie needed to make his decision so Pete could go ahead with plans for a general auction sale on the Overseth farm in the spring.

In March of 1905, the big move began. Johanna was now settled in her little house in Canton. It was located in the same block as Auntie Margarete Tetterud. For several weeks Johnny Overseth had been hauling loads of his mother's belongings into town. Now the Overseth house was empty, except for Christian Narum's room. He would be staying on to be the wood man for the Nordlies. Yesterday, March 14th, the Overseth auction sale had been held and now the barn and sheds were empty.

Today Ole and Helmina Nordlie had begun transporting their possessions to the Overseth homestead. The lumber wagons had been filled with furniture, the cookstove and cooking utensils, clothing, bedding and canned goods; and all day long they made the two-and-a-half-mile trip back and forth.

They had had plenty of help, with brother, John Overseth, and neighbor, August Johnson, assisting Nordlie and his hired man, Reinert Linde, and Uncle Chris.

The Grevlos family was waiting to get in as soon as Ole and Helmina moved out.

Finally, when it got dark, the family gathered at the kitchen table in their new home. The stovepipes had been put up early in the day and the cookstove was in use again. The beds had been reassembled so everyone would have a place to sleep tonight. Otherwise, boxes and furniture were stacked helter-skelter in the rooms. Tomorrow there would be more trips to haul the machinery and grain. Then when they got time, they would have to haul the hay.

Tonight the horses, milk cows, steers, pigs and chickens slept in their new quarters. Carlo, the dog, also had found his accustomed place behind the cookstove.

Tonight everyone was tired and even a little irritable. By afternoon, the temperature had gone up and the roads began to get muddy, which had made hauling more difficult.

"Bertha and I have all the beds made," Helmina informed them.

Bertha Blom was a young neighbor girl who had lost her parents and now would be living with Nordlies to help Helmina with all her work.

"Yah, we will all sleep well tonight," Nordlie predicted. "After the long day of lifting and carrying furniture and boxes, we'll appreciate our beds."

Helmina passed the cold roast and bread around, and filled Reinert's, Christian's, and Nordlie's cups with coffee.

Carlo came out from behind the stove, thinking it was time that he ate also. He walked around the table, hoping someone would give him a treat. Obed threw him a piece of his meat. Next, the dog approached Nordlie and Uncle Chris, who were sitting side by side. Christian never had cared much for dogs and scolded in an irritable tone, *"Go away! You are a 'stig' (bad) dog!"* Carlo lowered his head in a guilty stance. Nordlie directed the dog to go and lie down. Carlo, with his tail between his legs, headed for the outside door.

After the family had finished eating, Obed went to look for his dog. He couldn't find him in the house. The door had been left ajar, so he went outside and called, "Carlo, Carlo." Obed came back into the kitchen very disappointed.

"Papa, Carlo doesn't come."

"Oh, he's around. You'll see."

Obed got his mother and father to help him search for his dog, but finally they all had to give up and go to bed.

"We'll look for Carlo in the morning when it is light. It isn't cold out tonight, so he'll be alright."

The next morning Obed got up early to see if his dog had come back. But still no pet. The men began with their moving tasks again. Nordlie, Reinert and Christian each hitched a team to a lumber wagon and headed down the road to the Nordlie farm to load up the grain.

They filled the wagons with oats and corn from the bins and began the trip back to Overseth. But Nordlie decided he should stop and see if the Grevlos family had gotten settled. He rapped at the familiar back door and Klara opened it. As he stood talking to her in the kitchen, he heard a noise behind the cookstove. He turned to look as Obed's dog came out. The short, chubby dog trotted over to Nordlie, wagging his tail in a very excited manner.

Nordlie bent down and petted Carlos' head.

"Oh, nei, Oh nei. So this is where you have been, Carlo. Obed has been looking all over for you."

Nordlie was so relieved to see him. Carlo had returned to their former house the night before, walking the two and a half miles in the dark and scratching on the door . . . and the Grevlos family had let him in.

Nordlie knew how happy Obed would be when he returned with his precious pet. He hoped that this time the move would be successful.

"Come, Carlo, and I'll take you home."

Chapter XIX

66 **A** re we almost there, Papa?" asked four-year-old Thelma. Her eyes peered out from her winter bonnet, the soft angora trimming framing her little face. She sat on her mother's lap as the buggy headed for Canton. Squeezed in between her mother and father was her brother, Obed.

It was a cool April day. A raw wind was blowing; spring had not yet arrived. The family was still dressed in their winter clothes. A shawl was wrapped over their legs.

"It'll be awhile," answered her father, as he gave a shake to the reins. "We barely passed the Moe Store so we have a long ways to go." He glanced over at his daughter. "Why don't you close your eyes and when you wake up, we will be at Grandma's house." The trip to Canton took about an hour and a half, a long time for a little girl to sit still.

When the Nordlie buggy reached the south end of Canton, Ole directed the horses across the railroad tracks and north through Main Street, then north and east to Grandmother Johanna Overseth's home. Here Nordlie left Helmina, Obed and Thelma while he attended to his business. The main reason for the trip today was to pay the taxes. The taxes on his own farm had to be paid, even though he wasn't living on it. And then he had to see Pete Overseth about estate business.

"Greet Uncle Pete from me," Helmina called, as her husband shook the reins and headed downtown.

Johanna Overseth was so happy to see her daughter and grandchildren. When she lived on the farm, they visited several times a week. She had been ready and waiting for them for over an hour. Ever since Helmina had phoned several days ago, Johanna had been preparing for them. Yesterday she had baked *goro*, Obed and Thelma's favorite cookie.

Johanna now looked at her grandchildren. In just the month since she had moved to town, it seemed Thelma and Obed had grown taller.

Johanna escorted Helmina and the children inside. It didn't really feel like her house yet . . . but this was the way things were now, and she would make the best of it.

Johanna had the table set. The potatoes were boiling on the stove, and the meatballs and gravy were simmering in the oven.

After they had eaten dinner, Johanna suggested they take a little walk over to Auntie Tetterud's. By afternoon, the sun was shining and the temperature had risen.

"Auntie is always asking about you and the children, Helmina. She gets lonesome. It's hard for her to visit with people because of her hearing. She doesn't go out much."

They put on their coats and walked south to the corner and then east to the third house, located right across the street from the East Side School.

Helmina knocked at the door. They waited for an answer. Finally, Johanna suggested they go in. "Auntie doesn't hear well, you know."

Margrethe Tetterud was in the kitchen and she was both surprised and glad to see her guests. Right away she set the coffee pot on the stove, then she got out her hearing horn and sat down with Johanna and Helmina.

"*Are you going to stay a few days?*" she asked, as she pointed her hearing horn at Helmina.

"Oh, no." Helmina spoke in a loud voice. "We came with Nordlie. He's downtown."

"*Did Nordlie come along?*"

Helmina nodded her head, and almost shouting repeated, "Yes, Auntie. He's downtown doing some business."

"*Did he go downtown?*"

Helmina again nodded her head.

"Oh." There was a long pause while Margrethe Tetterud smiled as she slowly bent her head up and down to let them know she understood.

Helmina tried to think of a topic of conversation, but could think of nothing that didn't take a lot of explanation.

After an awkward pause, Auntie Tetterud again nodded her head and repeated her favorite old Toten expression, "*Yah, etter det det er!*" (Yes, that's the way it is!)

Thelma and Obed were restless. After rocking each other in the rocking chair, they explored the living room, looking at the pictures on the little table. Obed picked up a book lying there.

"*Nei,* be careful!" Auntie sternly instructed.

Obed turned to his mother and asked, "Can I go outside? I'll stay on the porch."

He put on his coat as his mother nodded her head.

Margrethe Tetterud decided to go out to the kitchen to check on the coffee.

"Don't fix much now, Auntie." Helmina spoke as she followed her. "Mother just made us a big dinner."

"Oh, you must have coffee and *berlinerkrandser* when you come to see me."

This little whisp of a lady kept on with her preparations. She got a chair to climb on so she could reach the top of her cupboard where she had her tin of *berlinerkrandser*. She arranged these cookies on a plate and set out her best cups and dishes.

Obed walked through the door to the porch. It faced the East Side School. It was recess and the children were outside playing. Obed sat down on the porch step and watched them.

Obed was now seven years old. He had had his birthday before Christmas and was old enough to go to school. However, with the moving this spring, it was decided to have him wait another year. Helmina had taught him herself; he could read and spell and work arithmetic, so he would be able to catch up next year.

"*Vaer saa god!*" (Be so good as to come to the table) Auntie loudly announced.

Johanna went to the porch to get Obed.

"Oh, you're watching the schoolchildren," she said. "If you lived in town, you could go to school there. Would you like that?"

"Yes, *Bestemor* (grandma). But I live in the country."

"Well, you could stay with me and keep me company, and then you could go to this school."

"Do you think I could?"

Johanna changed the subject. "Do you want a cookie? Auntie Tetterud has the lunch ready."

She took him by the hand and led him into the house.

Johanna, Helmina and the children barely got back to Johanna's when Nordlie drove up in the buggy.

"Can't you come in for a while?" Johanna invited.

"No, we'd better head for home. It's a long ride and I have a lot of chores to do."

Helmina and the children boarded the buggy and after waving goodbye to Johanna, they began their homeward journey.

"Did you get your business finished?" Helmina inquired.

"Yes. There were many people downtown today, especially ladies. Someone told me one of the hat shops was showing its new spring styles this week. You perhaps would have liked to see them too."

"Yes, I should go shopping one day, and it would have been interesting . . . but today mother really appreciated the time we spent with her. Anna is away visiting some of her college friends, and you know, Jim is in Brookings. Henry is gone so much of the time with school at Augustana, and mother said he has made so many new friends since they moved to town. Martin is working at the bank again, and is so busy with his music. I think Mother gets lonesome.

"By the way, we also visited Auntie Tetterud today."

"Papa, can I go to school in Canton?" Obed interrupted his parent's conversation. "Grandma said I could stay with her."

"What is this you say?" This idea didn't set very well with Ole Nordlie, who wanted his little family together.

He turned to Obed and asked, "What will the Johnson children say? They are looking forward to having you go along with them to the Rise School next year."

Now they were out in the country again. Ole Nordlie shook the reins, and with another "Geddap" he encouraged his team to increase their speed.

"Yah, Obed, it's a long time until fall. You'll get to go to school then, I promise. But we have plenty of time to make those decisions."

Ding! Dong! Ding! Dong! Ding! Dong! The Lands church bells rang out. It was the first Sunday in September, and it was time for the 11 o'clock services to begin. The ushers were setting up extra chairs in the back of the church because the pews were full, and latecomers were still tying up their horses and buggies outside.

Pastor Nummedal and the twenty-five members of the 1905 confirmation class marched in from the sacristy, the girls in new dresses and the boys in their first long trousers.

It was going to be another warm day. Sometimes the first week in September could be that way. The double doors in the entry had been left open, and all the windows were raised.

Sitting in the front row, just below the pulpit, was Ole Nordlie, the *klokker*. He got to his feet and faced the congregation to begin the Norwegian service.

"O Lord, our Maker, Redeemer, and Comforter, we have come together in Thy presence to hear Thy holy word . . ."

He knew this prayer well and needed no book. He stood with his hands folded, his clear voice carefully enunciating each word.

His next duty was to announce the first hymn and to lead in the singing of it. The members of the congregation got to their feet and everyone joined in the opening song of praise.

"Praise, my soul, the King of heaven,
To His feet thy tribute bring;
Ransomed, healed, restored, forgiven.
Evermore His praises sing!"

As he sang, he looked out at the many faces in the audience. Sitting on the men's side were his two hired men — Reinert Linde and Hans Rognlien. Hans Rognlien had just arrived in South Dakota this past week, and Ole was anxious to introduce him to his neighbors and friends today. Hans was a cousin of his brother-in-law in Norway, Otto Rognlien. He had immigrated from Hurdal the past spring and after four months in Wisconsin, Nordlie had hired him.

Every evening since Hans' arrival, Nordlie and Hans had sat up late visiting. Nordlie now could get information about all of his relatives and friends back in Hurdal.

Hans had described in detail the visit Marte Nordlien, his mother, had made to the Rognlien home several days before Hans left, so she could send special greetings to her son. It had touched Nordlie as Hans sat and repeated the things she had said.

"Tell Ole I still wait for his visit. It will be so special when he comes and I can see my two grandchildren and his wife."

Nordlie had questioned Hans thoroughly about his mother.

"Yes, your mother is well. She is just as little and energetic as ever, even if she is seventy years. But still I could tell she would really like to see you again."

Now Nordlie glanced at the confirmands in the front rows of the middle sections of the church. The boys sat on the north side of the middle aisle and the girls sat on the women's side, the south side.

One of the confirmands, Bertha Blom, had been living with them all year and was helping Helmina with the housework. Today she wore the new dress Helmina had been busy sewing.

Helmina had been up at 5 a. m. this morning, getting today's dinner prepared. They had invited Bertha's uncle and aunt, the John Skorheim family, and Bertha's brother, Brady, who lived with them. They also had invited their closest neighbors, the August Johnsons.

Now the congregation was finishing the last verse.

"Hallelujah, Hallelujah,
Praise the everlasting King."

Ole sat down again, and it felt good. He was tired, and his right foot had been bothering him lately—rheumatism or something. The service today would be very lengthy. On Confirmation Day, it always was.

Pastor Nummedal, in his flowing black gown with the accordian-pleated white collar, directed his confirmation class down the middle aisle to examine them. They stood in two rows, facing each other, the boys on the north side of the aisle and the girls on the south. Now the congregation would be able to see which students had learned their catechism.

Pastor Nummedal walked back and forth between the two lines and wisely chose the questions to fit the students—the difficult ones going to his best students. Then the class marched to the front of the church and stood in two rows to sing their class song.

Pastor Nummedal picked up his tuning fork and gave them the pitch. They would sing without accompaniment the way they did each week when the class met. Music and hymns were a very important part of the Christian life, and Pastor Nummedal had had them memorize many hymns. He had taught them to sing parts. Several of the boys were older and had already changed their voices and were able to sing bass.

They began the song, singing in the Norwegian language . . .

"Blessed Savior, who hast taught me
I should live to Thee alone;"

As Nummedal directed them, he looked into their faces and prayed that they were meaning the words they were singing.

Now he stepped up into the pulpit. It was time for the sermon. His kind eyes shone out from his bearded face. He cleared his voice and loudly began in Norwegian,

"COME, all you who are thirsty,
COME to the waters;
and you who have no money,
COME, buy and eat!" . . . Isa. 5:1

He looked at his audience and asked, "Are you thirsty?"

It was getting warm in the church with the many people packed tightly together. A cool drink of water would have been welcomed by all.

He continued. "You know that being thirsty is a serious matter. You can't live without water. You take your jug of water along when you go to the field. You are careful to see that your horses are watered several times a day, and you have a pan of water for the chickens and your dog.

"BUT there is a thirst that is more serious than thirst for water." He paused a moment and then emphasized, "It is a thirst for God!"

Pastor Nummedal put his arms on the pulpit and leaned toward his people, grasping the sides of the pulpit.

"KJAERE DERRE (My dear ones), and especially you confirmands, this thirst for God can't be quenched by money, good times, or even a big farm. Jesus himself says, *'If anyone is thirsty, let him come to ME and drink'.*"

Again, he leaned forward. A tear was running down his cheek. He pleaded, *"KJAERE DERRE, are you thirsty?* Do you have a longing to know Jesus better and to walk in His ways? Then Jesus says, *'Bare komme!* (Just come!)' "

This festive day also included communion, so it was two o'clock before Nordlie and Helmina and their household and guests returned home. After dinner the men set their chairs out on the south porch, and the topic that afternoon was the future government of Norway. The men were very concerned about it. Norway was separating from Sweden, and now the Norwegians would have to decide if their country would be a monarchy or a republic.

Skorheim and Nordlie were adamant that Norway should try a republic, and Uncle Chris and Reinert agreed. Swedish-born August also felt that was the best way to go. But to Hans Rognlien, a republic was as yet an unknown.

Yet no matter how determined these men felt about the rightness of a republic, none of them would ever have a vote in the matter.

Later in the afternoon, a buggy drove up with Martin, Tony and Anna Overseth. This farm was still home to them, and they dropped in often. Tony announced he had gotten a job clerking at the Lybarger Store in Canton. He would be selling shoes.

A houseful of guests wasn't a problem for Helmina who carried sandwiches, cake and cookies into the dining room for supper, and poured coffee while neighbors and relatives sat at the dining room table and visited.

Obed and Thelma Nordlie with their dog, Carlo.

Chapter XX

The warm weather of the first week in September soon changed and the rest of the month was rainy and chilly. This rain brought muddy roads and muddy fields. And the cool damp weather brought on colds and sickness.

Helmina came down with a bad cold. She even was bedfast for several days. It was fortunate Bertha's school hadn't begun, so Bertha could keep the household fed. This would be Bertha's final year at the Rise country school.

Obed had enrolled at the East Side School in Canton, and his school had begun the middle of September.

By October 2nd, Helmina was feeling better and the first thing she was going to do after her morning duties were out of the way was to write a letter to Obed. She was worried that he was getting homesick.

Helmina was pleased his schooling was working out so well. After being in the Canton school only a few weeks, the teacher had promoted him from primary to the first grade. Helmina was glad she had taught him well.

Hudson, S.D.
Oct. 2, 1905

My Dear Obed:

I am so sorry I could not come up to see you Friday, but you know it rained so and made the roads so bad that we could not come. Did you wait much for me?

I hope it will be nice weather Friday and Thelma and Mama will surely come up and take you home to your dear dogs. Won't that be nice?

Mama has not been well this last week. I have had a bad cold, but I hope to get better till Friday so I can go to Canton.

Well, Obed dear, I hope you are a good boy. Always remember that God can see and hear you everywhere, so never do or say anything that you don't want God to hear.

Thelma is well. She plays in the house all day; she is waiting so for you to come home.

All your dogs are O.K. Roy got a good whipping yesterday. He went about killing chickens so Reinert punished him, and I don't think Roy will do it again. Do you?

I guess I will have to stop my writing and get dinner for the men. Bertha started school today so Thelma and I are alone to do the work, you see.

Well Goodbye, Obed. Be a good boy. Write to us soon.

With much love from Papa, Thelma and

Mama

I put in 10 cents for you if you want to buy some little thing.

Helmina quickly addressed the envelope.

Master Obed Nordlie
Canton, S. Dak.
In care of Mrs. O. Overseth

She wanted to get it out to the mailbox before the mailman came by.

Helmina watered the fern that stood on the stand in the parlor. Then she picked up her dustcloth and dusted the carved corner table and the wooden rocking chair. Next she went to the organ—her father's organ—that had been left in the house. She lovingly dusted it while jabs of loneliness for him hit her. Oh, if only he was still here and she could see him sitting at his organ playing his favorite hymns.

Helmina was tempted to sit down and spend some time at the organ herself. This was how she relaxed, but that would have to wait until the day's work was finished.

Thelma was playing in the dining room with her little dishes and the cat. Helmina informed her she was going upstairs to clean and she should come along.

Helmina carried her cleaning supplies up the stairs and Thelma followed. Their first stop was the little room at the top of the stairs. This was now the hired man from Hurdal's room. Helmina made the bed and picked up his dirty clothes.

Thelma climbed up on one of the chairs. "*I want to look at Hans' horses.*" Hanging above the chair were several drawings of horses;

one was of a horse's head and mane, while the others showed the whole muscular animals. These were pictures Hans Rognlien had drawn. Before he immigrated he had worked for several years caring for horses in Norway. The owners of the Glass Factory at Hurdal included several well-to-do families and Hans' sole duty was to care for their fine horses. He groomed them, fed them, and kept the carriages clean and in good repair. When someone in the family was to go somewhere, it was his duty to drive them there.

Now Helmina picked up her dustcloth and dusted the chairs and the dresser. There, lying on the dresser was the letter Hans had received from his mother several days ago. Her husband, Ole, had been almost as happy as Hans to see the letter and to get to hear the news from Hurdal. It seemed to her that his longing for Norway and his old home had grown stronger since the new hired man came. She knew Ole was getting anxious to make a trip back to his native land . . . but he didn't talk about it. Her husband had been so very busy since they moved on her parents' farm that sometimes she feared he was working too hard.

After supper that evening, while Bertha did the dishes and the hired men read the papers, Ole Nordlie gathered the writing paper, pen and ink, and sat down at the dining room table to write letters to his loved ones back in Norway.

First, he wrote to his mother and told her Hans Rognlien had arrived and that Hans had given him her greetings. He was writing to reassure her, but putting it down on paper tended to reassure himself.

"Mother, I still am planning to come and bring my family to visit you. It shouldn't be very far off now, but I don't think it will be this next year. I am pretty tied down with all the animals and work on Helmina's father's farm. But I am making plans."

Then he wrote a letter to his brother-in-law and sister, Otto and Ingeborg Rognlien.

Moe, S.Dak.
Oct. 15, 1905

Dear Brother-in-Law Otto!
I have such bad rheumatism in my right foot tonight, but I will try to get something down on paper anyhow.
I have just been reading about the Union Affair in Norway and I thought I'd send a few words of what I thought about it while I

still am sane, and let you know what I think. Well, I suppose there is now peace and agreement. Now the question is "What sort of government will Norway choose?" If the people of Norway wanted to know what the Norwegians here in America wished, then Norway wouldn't go to a monarchy again. Now is the time for Norway to try something else. If the Norwegian people got a taste of being a Republic, then they wouldn't go back to a monarchy. In the first place, it is cheaper to have a republic form of government, and the great thing about it is that all the people can help decide for their own rights, and each individual can take an active part in their country's welfare.

Here the poorest people can advance to the top country's government positions, as well as the rich people. Here, for example, can I tell about our present President, Theodore Roosevelt? When he was young, he worked out west in the wilderness herding cattle, and riding horses. Now he is a man the whole world looks up to.

A sigh and a wish that is joint and common with all Norwegians here in this land is that "Oh, if only Norway would form a Republic!" Well, this must be all about this, Otto — I can't do anything about it, you know. But you who can must try what you can.

This summer we had a specially big crop of all kinds. We have just started to pick the corn. I can tell that Hans Rognlien has arrived here and I can greet you from him. He is now working for me.

I haven't much news to tell you, Otto, and I can't think about any either, as my wife is sitting and playing the organ so loud I'm quite dizzy in my head. Yes, and also a pain in my stomach from the noise. I have also written home to Mother today. I haven't had any letter from Hurdalen for quite a while. How are things there? Has Mathilda had her wedding yet? I became so ANGRY when I read in your letter that she was marrying a man from Skruklia that my wife nearly fainted, and the children began to cry. What is Mathilda thinking about? She surely isn't going to move there and live in such a dump, a place where one never sees folks except once a year. I don't know the man, but I can guess he is one with RED HAIR just like all the other Skruklendings have. If she isn't married yet, please ask Ingeborg to give her some advice, that she doesn't move there. I wish I could get her to come over here, then she wouldn't have to live like a hermit all her days.

I must close for now, and I expect a letter from you, Otto, for Christmas. Greet your wife and children, also Ludvig and wife. Hearty greetings from me and mine.

Yours,
Ole Nordlie

128

Professor Indseth and his Fairview Band. Indseth, in the center of the third row, with baton; Tony Overseth, back row, third from right, with trombone; Martin Overseth, second row, second from right, with cornet; Anton Stikbakke, second row, far left, and his brother, Hans Stikbakke, third from left, both with clarinets.

Chapter XXI

Wednesday, November 15th, 1905 brought sunshine. It turned out to be a nice day for a parade. Helmina was happy about that. Today Ole Nordlie had taken his wife and daughter along into Canton for Professor Indseth's Musical Jubilee. The Moe Band would be participating. And not only that! The Canton school children would be marching in the parade.

Hundreds of teams and buggies were in town today, and people were beginning to gather along Main Street.

Ole decided to treat his daughter to ice cream while waiting for the parade. They crossed Main Street and headed for the drug store, but the window of the Syverud and Moe Jewelry Store caught his eye and he stopped several minutes to look at the display of rings, silverware and watches.

Long chains were attached to some of the watches so they could be worn around the neck. That was very fashionable for the ladies now. Nordlie was looking for ideas for a Christmas gift for Helmina. He thought she would like that.

"Come on, Papa," Thelma tugged at his trouser leg. He took her hand, and they headed next door to the drug store. Today Thelma had on her angora trimmed bonnet and carried her little angora muff. Last night Helmina had rolled her daughter's hair up on rags so she had long locks hanging below her bonnet. Ole was proud of his little girl and enjoyed watching as the people noticed her.

The Noid Drug Store was crowded. Many other people had had the same idea as he. Nordlie walked up to the beautiful marble soda fountain with the large mirrored back and ordered a little dish of ice cream for the two of them. Nordlie was always impressed with the Noid Drug Store's elegant furnishings.

Ole's thoughts returned to the news Helmina's mother had given them that forenoon. Helmina's brother, Martin, was going to be a storekeeper. He was buying a small variety store, "The Fair," located in the east part of downtown, near the Rudolph Hotel. He hoped to open for business a month from now. Ole had seldom traded there because he usually patronized only the stores run by Norwegians. Yah, Ole figured, Martin will soon be getting his inheritance and so would have money for this enterprise.

As Thelma was taking the last bites of ice cream, Ole could hear the faint sounds of band music. It was time to move. When they got outside, he could see the procession two blocks away on South Main. He picked up Thelma and quickly crossed the street and entered the Puckett-Pidcoe Company where Helmina and Johanna were shopping. The store was being remodeled, and a thirty-five foot addition was being added in the rear area. He could hear hammering and sawing going on in the back room. When the renovations and decorating were finished, Puckett-Pidcoe was to be a magnificent department store. Business had been very good lately, and today it was full of customers.

Ole hurried the ladies along. They were selecting dress material. *"We'd better get outside because the bands are coming!"* After all, that was why they had come to town today. They all found a spot in front of the Puckett-Pidcoe building. People were lining up all along Main Street and also along Fifth Street.

The music was getting louder. As the four bands came nearer, marching to a lively air, he could see the parade was headed by a platoon of guardsmen as an escort, under the command of Lieutenants Way and Eneboe.

The Inwood, Harrisburg, Moe and Canton bands followed, united under the proud leadership of Professor Andrew Indseth. People clapped as the director went by. Indseth was dressed in a solid black uniform, with his white shirt and bow tie. His unique but distinguished-looking beard sort of swirled around his lips and chin in all directions.

The sidewalks downtown were lined with people who came to see the procession of handsome musicians in their fine uniforms.

The bands were right alongside them now. Ole held Thelma up so she could see. Finally, he caught sight of the Moe Band. There was Martin with his trumpet, Tony with his trombone, and Helmina's cousin, Anton Bakke (Stikbakke), with his clarinet. Anton had emigrated from Norway this past year and was working as a hired man in the Moe community. Ole knew all the members of the Moe Band because they were his neighbors.

The column wheeled west on Fifth Street, now playing a peppy march. When in front of Segrud's Gallery, the group halted and the entire instrumental organization filed inside to have pictures taken.

Helmina and her mother went back inside the store to finish their shopping while Ole visited with people standing along the curb, all the while keeping an eye on Segrud's Gallery.

About a half hour later, the bands filed out of the photo gallery and with an added escort of over four hundred school children, they marched down Bartlett and east on Sixth Street.

Ole and his group went south to Sixth Street where they could get a good look at everyone in the parade. Helmina and Ole kept watching for Obed, who would be walking with his classmates. Helmina was the first to spy him. There he was in his knickers and coat, cap and mittens. They all waved at him, but he kept a very serious face, looking straight ahead.

It still was only a little after one o'clock, so Ole guided Helmina, Johanna and Thelma south to where his buggy was tied. The parade was to continue east and north until it finally came back to the Opera House on Fifth Street.

Ole and Helmina brought Johanna home, where she was to care for Thelma while they attended the afternoon concert. Ole and Helmina hurried back downtown. Now Ole brought his team to the livery stable where Bessy and Queen could munch on hay, and be more comfortable for the several hours until they would be returning home.

The afternoon program at the Opera House began at two o'clock. The building was jammed with relatives and friends of the band members. By the time Ole and Helmina got there, the seventy-two musicians were tuning up.

Nordlie sat back in his seat, anticipating an enjoyable afternoon. There was something exciting about marching bands, all the musicians, and all the people . . . and to top it off, John G. Erikson of Sioux Falls was to deliver an address on "New Norway."

Ole wasn't disappointed. The concert was outstanding. Indseth's music was always good. What this man had done with these farm and small town boys and men was almost unbelievable. He had a way of bringing the music out of them, that was for certain.

The bands played many marches, and several numbers which Indseth himself had composed. Before the speaker, the band played Grieg's impressive *"Hall of the Mountain King,"* which Indseth had arranged.

Mr. Erickson spoke on Norway's new monarchy. Ole still was a little disappointed at Norway's decision. He and most Norwegian-Americans had hoped Norway would decide for a republic. A vote had been taken and the Norwegians wanted a king. They had approached the royal family of Denmark and now would be getting a prince from there for their king.

After the speech, Indseth soloed on his violin in Ole Bull's "*Seter-jenten's Sondag*." Again Ole became absorbed in this melancholy melody. It was beautiful and sad at the same time. It was as if an invisible chord was pulling him back to his homeland. The memories flooded in. He could picture Snultra, the seter high up on Nordli Kampen mountain, the Hurdal church down in the valley, and the crystal clear Hurdal Lake.

His thoughts went back to his mother and his sisters and brothers in Norway. This was his kind of music. He seemed part of it and it seemed part of him.

After the concert was over, Ole and Helmina returned to Johanna's. Obed was home from school now and Johanna insisted they have lunch before they headed home. The coffee was simmering on the back of the stove and she already had arranged a plate of sandwiches and cookies.

Soon Martin and Tony joined them.

"Well, folks, what did you think about the concert?" Martin asked.

Nordlie assured them he had enjoyed it immensely.

"You should stay for tonight and the grand finale," Martin advised. "Besides the four bands, tonight the *Wendt orchestra* of Canton will join us, and also two men's choruses, the *Minnehaha Mandskor* from Sioux Falls, and the *Canton Grieg Sangforening*. Indseth directs us all."

"Yah," Tony explained, "that Indseth is a busy man. He travels weekly by buggy and train all over the area to practice at all these places. He and his family recently moved to Fairview, but he's always there at Moe for our practice nights."

Martin added, "And tonight we will all join together to play Indseth's new composition, 'The Midnight Sun,' which he has dedicated to Norway. It is outstanding! You must stay and hear THAT!"

Ole felt disappointed at having to miss it, but explained, "If I lived in Canton, I would surely be there, but driving home late at night isn't for me . . . and Thelma will be too tired. I guess we'll have to be satisfied with the fine music we heard this afternoon."

"Say, Hemmy," Martin questioned his sister, "did you hear I'm going to be a storekeeper?"

"Yes, Mother was telling us about it. That will keep you busy, Martin."

"I'm really glad the city fathers voted to shorten the city's store hours. All the stores will close at eight o'clock from now on. That is, except the drugstores. That means we will have the evenings free for our music.

And there's a big room back of the store where we can get together at nights and practice. Did Mother tell you Tony and I had rented the sleeping room above the store? That will be real handy."

All the way home, Ole Nordlie had a melody running through his head. He began humming it as the horses trotted along the road towards home.

"I gaze on the sun as it mounts in the sky,
It soon will be time for Gudsjeneste (church services).
I wish I were home to follow along
AS folks wend their way to the kirke (church).

The tune of *"Seterjenten's Sondag"* still had a hold on him.

Chapter XXII

Snow as fluffy and delicate as bits of cotton brushed against Ole Nordlie's face as he headed for the barn on this winter day in the middle of December, 1905. It had been snowing during the night and now the dark, shabby fall landscape had taken on a clean look. The snow descended without wind or wintry cold and it was beautiful. It lay in little piles on each fencepost and on the wooden fences and topped the corncribs and sheds like white frosting.

The snow didn't bother Ole today. Last week he and the hired men had finished the corn picking, the cattle yards had fresh straw piled over the frame sheds, and the upstairs of the barn was filled with hay. *Yah, let winter come,* he thought.

As he approached the barn, Ole met his hired man, Hans Rognlien, who had finished the milking. Hans set down the two pails of milk he was carrying and the two men stood and admired the falling snow.

"Doesn't this remind you of Norway, Ole?" Hans asked.

"Yah, it isn't often we get snow without wind in South Dakota," Ole answered.

"If it gets much deeper, we can go on skis," Hans remarked. "By the way, Ole, have you got a pair of skis around here?"

"No, Hans. This just isn't skiing country, and I never bought a pair."

"Back home in Hurdal we MADE skis. I remember watching *Far* (Father) make a pair for me when I was about Obed's age."

"Yah, I remember my father making a pair for my sister. Back home everyone traveled with skis. When the snow got deep, it was the best way to get around. We had a pair of little skis my sisters used almost as soon as they could walk."

"I really miss going on skis. This snow makes me long for it even more."

Ole was quiet for a few moments as they both watched the big fluffy flakes descend.

"*You know, it's a SHAME*," Nordlie sadly commented.

Hans turned to look at him, then asked, "What's a shame?"

"Why, Hans, here I have two children. Obed will be eight years old next week, and he's never been on skis. *That's a shame*! He has Norwegian blood in him, too, and he's never had a chance to ski."

"I agree with you. A child with Norwegian blood in his veins should have a pair of skis. Say, Ole, why don't you make him a pair for Christmas? I'll help you.

"That's not a bad idea. I think I have some fine pieces of lumber that we could use. We can get a good fire going in the old stove out in the washhouse and use Helmina's wash boiler. I can still see Father standing over the steaming big kettle working with the wooden skis."

"If I remember right, first we have to cut out the skis and sand the edges so they are nice and smooth, and then we will have to spend several days soaking them in boiling water until they are pliable enough to bend," Hans recalled.

"That's right, Hans. Between the two of us, I think we can do it. When I go to Canton I'll get strapping and buckles to hold them on."

Hans looked around at the snow-covered scenery. "Yah, what is snow without skis? Say, Ole, if the pair for Obed turns out well, maybe we can make a pair that we can use."

Several days later, Ole and Helmina Nordlie made a trip to Canton. It was getting close to Christmas and they would try to finish their shopping.

"Could we stop at Martin's new store?" Helmina asked. "His ad said he carries a few groceries too. I can just as well get the things I need from him."

Martin, in his white grocer apron, was busy waiting on customers. This was a good time of the year to begin his store business. Today the town was full of people buying supplies and gifts for Christmas. Martin carried some men and women's clothes and tables of 5, 10, and 15 cent merchandise. People from the Moe community were especially curious to see his new business.

Helmina couldn't find all of her supplies at Martin's so she finished her shopping at the big grocery store run by Chraft and Hanson, where they kept all kinds of Norwegian supplies . . . cardamom, lingonberries and lutefisk — a place where you could shop even if you spoke only the Norwegian language.

There was a hurried excitement in the air today as everyone was getting ready for Christmas. Helmina stopped at Puckett's for some cloth and trimmings so she could finish the Christmas dresses she was making for Bertha and Thelma, and some yarn for mittens she was knitting for the hired men.

Ole went to the Farmers State Bank to see Uncle Pete about the farm estate business.

"Nordlie," Pete informed him, "when February comes, we'll be distributing the Overseth estate. I figure each of the children will get a little over $1600 from the cash in the estate. I was wondering if Helmina would want to invest her share in some land. I just heard that Tollefsrud, who moved back to Minnesota, is interested in selling his two eighties that run through the middle of the section east of your farm. Johanna should invest some of her money in land also. She'll be getting over $5,000. She could buy the south eighty, and you and Helmina the eighty lying north of it. This should be handy for you, just a half mile from your farm."

"I agree. That would be a good investment for us. I'll talk it over with Helmina and let you know. It's her inheritance, you know."

After their errands and their Christmas shopping, they drove to Johanna's to pick up Obed and head for home, ready to finish their projects for Christmas.

Obed greeted them at Johanna's door.

"Mama! Papa! Guess what the teacher told me today."

Both Ole and Helmina looked perplexed. They didn't know if it was good or bad. Then Helmina glanced at her mother who was standing behind Obed. She had a big smile on her face. Finally Helmina answered, "It must be something good."

"Yes, Mama. Today is the last day of school, and when I come back after Christmas vacation, the teacher said I'd be in the second grade."

They both looked at him with pride. Their son was doing well in school.

Christmas 1905 would always be known as *"The Bachelor's Christmas."* Around the table on *Julekveld* (Christmas Eve) were the two hired men, Hans Rognlien and Reinert Linde, who both had become part of the family, and Uncle Chris Narum, the wood man, and Uncles Pete and Hans Overseth. Pete had taken the train to Hudson where Hans Overseth had a room in the hotel, and the two of them had driven the five and a half miles to the Overseth farm with horse and buggy. Then there was Helmina's cousin, Anton Stikbakke, who had been working in the community.

Helmina and Bertha carried in platters of *"ribbe"* (pork ribs), and lutefisk and lefse, and bowls of potatoes, melted butter, lingonberries and carrots . . . and refilled them again and again. The men all ate well.

After finishing with the different Norwegian cakes and cookies, the men pulled their chairs into the corner of the dining room while Helmina and Bertha cleared the table.

Uncle Pete leaned back in his chair. He gave a contented sigh. *"Ribbe!* That was delicious, Hemmy."

"We always had 'ribbe' on Julekveld back home," Nordlie explained.

Anton spoke up. This was the first Christmas he had been away from home. "I'll wager my mother is fixing '*ribbe*' back home tonight."

The men all found relaxing positions; some stretched out their legs or leaned their chairs back in a balancing, rocking position. They were all well satisfied and the mention of '*ribbe*' brought back memories of their childhood Christmases in Norway. It was quiet as they each had their own thoughts. Nordlie broke the silence.

"When we were children there at home, we would sit in the evenings and figure out how long it was until Christmas arrived."

Hans interrupted . . ."and then the malting man came, and a couple of weeks later there was butchering and the ale was started."

Uncle Pete added . . ."and then Mother was baking for days on end with breads and cakes and cookies."

Uncle Hans, who always was so quiet, began to share. "I remember the first Christmas after Marianne and I were married and we were living in Valdres, away from relatives, but she fixed '*ribbe*' and lefse and potatoes for just us two."

Hans Overseth's wife had died several years after that, and he had immigrated to the United States where his brothers, Peter and Ole Overseth, lived, and clerked in Pete's store in Hudson.

Nordlie went on, "And then came Christmas Eve. How happy we children were when mother was cooking the Christmas Eve food and Father set a *"karafel"* of ale on the table."

Again it was quiet as the men were each with their thoughts.

"No, we'll never forget the Christmases of our childhood." Nordlie summed it up for them all.

Obed and Thelma interrupted their reminiscing.

"Papa, it's time to light the tree," they reminded him. Ole got up right away, for who had less patience than children on Christmas Eve? He still could remember that.

Nordlie fetched the matches, and as everyone watched closely, he lit all the candles on the Christmas tree. It was a beautiful sight, but all the adults were very much aware of the danger of fire that went with it. Ole set a pail of water alongside the packages in case of an emergency.

Nordlie stood by the tree as he read the Christmas story. The bright glittering tree made a good background for the story of the star and the angels. And because Ole knew most of it by memory, he could keep his eye on the burning candles.

Obed then recited the poem he would give the next night at the Sunday School Christmas program in church. This year Thelma, who was almost five, also had a line to speak. Then everyone sang. These bachelor men perhaps didn't know many songs, but they each knew all the verses of "*Jeg er saa glad hver Julekveld*" (I am so glad each Christmas Eve).

Uncle Pete had brought gifts for the children. Thelma opened hers first. It was a beautiful doll, with a china head and real hair, clothed in a lovely dress. Thelma hugged her. "Thank you, Uncle Pete. I think I'll call her *Pearl*." Helmina had read her a story about a doll with that name.

Obed opened Uncle Pete's gift and found a complicated little steam engine. When benzine was put in it, and the boiler filled with water, and it was lit, the engine would run and steam would come out. This interested all the men and they all hovered around Obed and his interesting toy.

Nordlie then went out by the back door and carried in a very long skinny package, which had been wrapped in brown paper. He gave it to Obed. It was the skis Hans and he had made. They had turned out well.

"*Do you think you can stand up on those*?" Hans teased Obed. Obed could hardly wait until the next morning so he could go outside and find out.

Helmina and Ole picked up the wrapping papers and Helmina, with her new fashionable watch hanging around her neck, passed oranges, apples and nuts; then she served more cookies and coffee. The men who had come from Norway went to bed with memories from both this Christmas and their childhood Christmases in Norway still in their heads.

Coffee time on the Nordlie lawn. **Ole Nordlie in foreground, holding cup of coffee. Helmina, and brother, Tony Overseth, in background, and young Obed in front.**

Chapter XXIII

Helmina Nordlie lifted the cream can into the buggy and climbed in. Today Uncle Chris had hitched Bessy with one of the younger horses, and the team was standing ready and waiting for her.

She sat down on the seat and pulled the cream can close to her legs, then picked up the reins, gave them a shake, and with a "geddap," headed the horses down the long driveway. Today she would get some baking supplies she needed at the Moe Store.

The April day was chilly so she flung her shawl over her head and turned up her coat collar. Helmina was troubled today. She had gotten news this morning that the daughter of her friend and neighbor had died. Little Cora Steensland was only a few months older than Obed. Her heart went out to Ida. How it must hurt. She could just imagine how terrible it would be if it had been Obed or Thelma.

Two weeks earlier, Helmina and Thelma had driven Bessy over to visit the Steenslands. Ida and her auctioneer husband lived about a mile west of the Lands Church. Helmina hadn't let Thelma go into the house. That tuberculosis was a bad insidious disease. She had watched it take all the sparkling life out of sweet eight-year-old Cora. And this sickness had a way of spreading. Thelma had played outside in the swing with Hazel, who was near Thelma's age. One good thing was that John and Ida had other girls to comfort them.

Helmina had decided to bring some food over for the Steenslands to use for the lunch after the funeral. That was why she was making this trip to the store this morning. She would bake a white cake and make some sandwiches. That was the least she could do.

Helmina's attention returned to her team of horses. It was almost time to turn and go west to the Moe corner. The horses were going a little faster than she liked, so she tightened the reins and then pulled on the left rein to turn them west to the store.

Everytime the horses turned a corner, Helmina had to hold on to the cream can that sat by her legs. When the team made this quick turn, the cream can started sliding toward the open side of the buggy. She grabbed for it! But in the process of turning, both she and the cream can fell from the buggy.

It took place so fast, Helmina hardly knew what was happening. She screamed *"whoa,"* but Lady became nervous and plunged forward. Worse still, the reins had been twisted around Helmina's legs and she was being dragged.

Helmina was scared. She hollered, *"BESSY! WHOA! WHOA!"* If the horses started running, she didn't know where she would end up. Suddenly the buggy came to a stop. Bessy had her four feet firmly planted on the ground and was holding Lady back. When Helmina realized the horses had finally stopped, she untangled herself from the reins and managed to get to her feet. None of her bones seemed to be broken, but she was very shook up.

She picked up the empty can and its cover and put it back in the buggy. All the nice thick cream was on the ground . . . and on her clothes!

Now Helmina was almost crying. She tried to hold back the sobs because she didn't want to scare that young horse any more. She was trembling as she climbed back into the buggy. She straightened out the reins, turned the team around and returned home.

When Bertha and Thelma saw Helmina drive up, they thought it was strange she was back so soon, and they came outside to see what was the matter.

Helmina was still shaking as she got down from the buggy. All the way home, all she could think of was . . ."*If it hadn't been for Bessy! If it hadn't been for Bessy!*"

Helmina tied the team to the hitching post. Now she took time to pet Bessy's head as she quietly sobbed, *"Thank you, Bessy."* Five-year-old Thelma was upset to see her mother cry, and she began to cry also.

Helmina limped toward the house, still sobbing. She was certain God had sent one of his guardian angels to hold Bessy's bridle and keep her from moving. There was no other reasonable explanation. She realized how dangerous her situation had been and how she had been saved from what could have been her death.

After supper that night, Ole Nordlie made the trip to Moe Store and got the ingredients Helmina needed for her baking the next day. And he told the men who were sitting there visiting about how his faithful white horse Bessy had been a heroine that forenoon.

During the summer of 1906, there were many church gatherings in the Moe community. On May 20th, the beautiful new Trinity Church, which was located in the same section as the Overseth farm, was dedicated, and hundreds of people came for the festivities. The sanctuary leveled in the 1902 tornado, had now been rebuilt. The Nordlies' neighbors, the August Johnsons, were members there, and Ole and Helmina and family attended the dedication.

On Sunday, June 10th, 1906, Helmina was up very early. This was the day the Lands church would celebrate its 30th Anniversary by gathering after services for a picnic dinner on the parsonage lawn. Helmina planned to fry chicken before going to the 11 a.m. services. Ole was outside now killing the chickens and she was getting the water boiling so they could clean and defeather them.

Ole had been up first and had a good fire going in the cookstove. She was glad she had gotten her mince pies ready yesterday. Yesterday Helmina's mother, Johanna, had come out with Ole when he made a trip to Canton. Johanna was one of the early members of Lands, and everyone insisted that she attend.

While Helmina was working, her thoughts drifted to her father, Ole Overseth. How he would have enjoyed this day. He loved getting together with neighbors and friends and the Lands Church always had meant so much to him.

Today everyone, except Uncle Chris, would be going to church. Johanna, Bertha and Thelma rode in the surrey with Ole and Helmina, and the two hired men took Obed with them.

There were many of the older members who had made a special effort to attend today. Also, former members who had moved to Canton, made the trip out. All the seats in church were filled. There was a feeling of excitement and rejoicing today. The choir presented several numbers and the congregation sang a hymn.

Nummedal ascended into the pulpit to begin his sermon. His kind eyes looked over his congregation. Sitting out there were both the young and the old. He opened the big Bible and began, "I would like to read from Joshua, chapter I, today.

'*As I was with Moses, so I will be with thee;*
I will never fail thee nor forsake thee.'

"On the occasion of this anniversary, we look back to see how God has led the Lands congregation for these thirty years. Babies have been born and baptized, children have been taught the Word, young people have confirmed their faith in Jesus, and the Word has gone forth at each service to be imbedded in hearts and to change lives. God has been with the Lands congregation.

"But now many of the charter members have gone on, just as Moses had in this text. Yet God still had work to be done. In those days He turned this assignment over to Joshua and the next generation.

"Now God speaks these same words to the next generation of the Lands congregation. He still has work to be done here. There is an inheritance to be claimed. This inheritance is not land . . . but SOULS in this community."

He firmly gripped the pulpit with both hands and leaned toward the congregation.

"*KJAERE DERRE. Do you want to be blessed, and do you want to be a blessing*? Then I challenge you, Lands congregation, go forth with God's Word and claim your inheritance. God will be with you."

After the benediction, everyone crossed the road north of the church and gathered on the large parsonage lawn. Mrs. Nummedal and some of the other women were making coffee, and several of the men were pumping good cold water for the lemonade. Quilts were spread out on the lawn and people sat in groups to share their food. Children were running here and there. After the meal, men and women moved around and visited.

Ed Linde and Albert Hegnes had driven their new auto up from Beresford, and after the meal it proved to be the main attraction. Ed Linde had been an important member of this community for many years as he had first clerked in the Moe Store, and then he and Adolph Gubbrud bought the store from Knute Jacobson and Claus Hegnes.

This new invention with wheels had a big windshield in front, but had no top like the buggies did, and only half doors. It was a noisy machine, especially when the engine backfired.

Ole Nordlie had read in the Canton paper about the ride Ed and Albert had given Knute Jacobson in Canton a couple of weeks ago. That day Knute had a difficult time trying to keep his ten-inch rim straw hat on as the auto sped down the road at thirty miles an hour.

And Ole had heard how dangerous these machines were on the narrow highways. They would scare the teams of horses and cause runaways. People and buggies often ended up in the ditches. Many people who met these autos would shake their fists at them.

"Well, Ole," Ed said, as he proudly looked at his automobile, "what do you think of it? It's the coming thing! And Beresford is becoming the car capital. It already had sixteen autos, with two more ordered, and I don't think Canton has one yet."

"Yah, Ed," Ole replied. "It is quite a machine, but you young sports can have your autos. I'll stick with Bessy and my horses."

The Nordlie household sat around the breakfast table with heads bowed as Ole Nordlie finished the prayer at the end of the Norwegian morning devotions. Helmina and Bertha carried in the dishes of oatmeal, and poured the coffee, then passed the bread, butter and jelly. The milking and early chores were finished and the horses harnessed, all ready for another work day.

Hans Rognlien was very excited this morning. "Do you realize that this is June 24th, the day that Norway gets its own King and Queen?"

He paused, and slowly added . . ."KING HAAKON, the 7th! How does that sound?"

Nordlie had visions of the grand occasion too. "With the time difference, I suppose they have already had the coronation," he said.

"You can bet they '*gjøre stas*' (make a festive mood) in Trondjheim today!" Hans pointed out.

"Yah," Nordlie agreed, "now Norway has a King and Queen, but I still think she should have decided on a democracy . . . with a President."

The men got busy with their food and then the subject changed. Reinert wanted to know what the plans were for the day.

"Reinert, you keep on with the corn cultivating in the field along the driveway, . . . and Hans, you can mow the hayfield over on the west eighty."

Nordlie took a drink of coffee. "I must make a trip to Hudson today for some lumber and other things we need to make some repairs around here. We have to keep things in good shape."

He turned to his wife, "Helmina, are there some things you need in Hudson?"

"No, I don't think so. I want to make a trip to Canton later this week. You know Martin is selling out his merchandise at reduced prices, and I can probably find some good buys there. There's nothing I need in Hudson."

On the mention of Martin's store, Nordlie commented. "Yah, Martin's storekeeping didn't last very long. I guess there was too much competition in Canton. Even after he moved all of his merchandise to the building on Main Street in March, it still didn't go well."

Hans added, "It looks to me like about every other store in Canton is selling the same things—overalls, thread, underwear . . . and groceries!"

The men got up from the table and went out to get on with their work. Ole Nordlie washed and shaved, put on clean overalls and hitched Bessy and Queen to the lumberwagon.

It was a fine June day. The grass was green again, and as he drove down the lane, he took in the beautiful sight of the acres of newly cultivated corn along the driveway. Reinert was directing the team up and down the straight rows, leaving the strips of freshly turned black dirt to contrast the bright green corn plants.

Ole turned east towards Hudson, and after he passed the August Johnson driveway, he saw August standing by the road fence. August was yelling to him, *"Are you going to Hudson*?"

"Yes," Nordlie hollered back.

"Kjøpe meg sukkerbitta." (Buy me some sugar lumps.)

Ole Nordlie thought he said "Buy me some baby socks," so he asked, "What color do you want? black or brown?"

August was puzzled at that question.

"Nei, Nordlie. *Nei, sukkarbitta for kaffien."* (sugar lumps for the coffee)

"Oh." Now Nordlie understood.

"Yah, August, I'll get sugar lumps."

August's Swedish dialect often confused Nordlie.

August climbed back on his cultivator, and headed his team of mules down the corn rows. Nordlie glanced at August's field. Yes, it was the same as always—*wavy rows*, where his mules had balked when he had planted the corn. But it didn't seem to bother August.

Nordlie shook his reins, and with a "Geddap" continued his trip to Hudson.

In the store in Hudson, there was a lot of advertising about activities for the Fourth of July, which would be here soon. Since this was the first year Hans Rognlien had been in America, Nordlie decided he would like to show him how they celebrated here. He purchased a case (24 bottles) of pop for the Fourth, with strawberry, grape, orange and creme soda. He also bought fireworks—little firecrackers for the children, and rockets and Roman candles to use in the evening.

On his way home, he stopped at the Johnsons with the *"sukkarbits,"* and invited August and family to come over the afternoon of the Fourth and have supper with them, and see the fireworks. Yes, he would show Hans that he was patriotic.

The morning of July 4th, the children were up early and began shooting the little ladyfingers, but Curl, the black dog that had come to their place last fall, went wild.

They had tried to find the dog's owner, but couldn't, and the animal had attached himself to Obed and Thelma as their protector.

When the children began to shoot the firecrackers, the dog wanted to keep them from the dangerous noisy things, and put the lit firecrackers in its mouth. And then it would howl with pain. But they couldn't get the dog away from the children.

Thunder and lightning were the dog's other fears, and with the first thunder peal, the dog always headed for the barn or shed.

In the afternoon the Johnsons came over. The older children, Hermand and Anna, had other plans. After the little firecrackers were used up, the Johnson girls and Thelma went inside where Helmina and Maria were getting the supper on the table. The girls decided to go upstairs to play. There was a trunk full of old clothes and curtains that Thelma could use for dress-up.

Today the older girls decided they would play wedding. Ruth would be the bride and a lace curtain would be her train. There were some old cloth flowers and old hats that the other girls put on. But, they decided, they needed a groom.

"Thelma, go and get Obed. He'll be just right for the groom. He can wear this old black derby hat and this man's suitcoat. And he can carry this cane." Esther gave the instructions.

Thelma didn't know if she could get him, but she was persuaded to try. Obed was on the lawn, petting Curl, who was worn out from the difficult day.

"Obed, will you come in and play with us?"

"With you girls?"

"We need you. You can wear Papa's old black hat and his coat."

"It's too hot to dress up."

"Oh, come on. We need you."

The reluctant brother followed his sister inside and upstairs where the bridal party was assembling.

When he saw they were playing wedding, he protested. "No! No! No!"

"Oh, come on. It won't hurt you," Esther, the older Johnson girl, told him. "Thelma and Judith will be flower girls. I will be the bridesmaid."

Finally he slipped on Papa's coat. They gave him the hat, which was too big, but he put it on and carried the stylish cane. He felt quite grown-up, even if he was only going to be in the third grade.

Judith called from the top of the staircase and told her mother and Helmina to come and watch. They were in the dining room, putting food and dishes on the table. They turned two chairs around and sat down to watch.

Down the staircase they came. First came Thelma and Judith in their big hats, carrying flowers, and humming, *"Here Comes the Bride."* Following in the procession was Esther with a beautiful beflowered hat, and then came Ruth with the lace curtain that was pinned to her hair and dragging on behind. She carried a large spray of flowers, and Obed in his formal attire was by her side.

Maria Johnson was beside herself with *"Oh's"* and *"Aah's."*

"Oh, see! Oh, see, Helmina! Obed and Rute, isn't that sweet?"

She began to clap and then she turned to Helmina and became very serious. "This isn't so far off, Helmina. Why, one day it could well happen like this."

When Obed heard that, he threw off the coat and hat and laid down the cane and ran out the door to sit on the lawn with August, Nordlie and the hired men, where it was safer.

And on the Fourth of July, 1906, all the pop was drunk up, and later all the fireworks were shot off, and Hans Rognlien got to see an American holiday.

One of the new automobiles. Tony Overseth behind the wheel. Ole Nordlie is seated in the rear — Circa 1909.

Chapter XXIV

Helmina had gotten the wash on the line early, and with the warm August breeze, at 11 o'clock she decided she would check to see if the clothes were dry. Bertha was peeling the potatoes and the meat was in the oven, so there would be time to bring the clothes in from the clothesline before the men came in for dinner.

Helmina carried her clothespin pail and clothes basket along out with her. Everything was dry except the overalls and rugs. She began taking the sheets off the line, folding them and placing them in the basket. She would get the clean sheets back on the beds this afternoon. Tonight everyone could enjoy the fresh bedding. It took a lot of sheets for all the beds in her farm family.

But it was a lovely day. The breeze had a cool touch to it. She decided this was the best part of washday — taking down the clothes that smelled so good, and feeling pride in the whiteness of the men's shirts and the big tablecloth. There was nothing like the sun and good strong homemade soap to make them white.

She was distracted from her thoughts by the sound of a motor. It must be out on the highway, she decided. She took down several more shirts, and then she realized it was coming up their lane. Helmina walked to the front of the house to see what was coming . . . and it was, as she feared, one of those new automobiles.

When it came closer, it began to slow up, with loud pop-pops as it backfired. The chickens, in great fear, flew up and out of the way, and the horses standing by the barn kicked up their hind legs and ran off to the pasture. Only a few curious old milk cows stood by the barn, looking on at this noisy monster that had pulled into the yard.

Now Helmina saw who the driver was! Martin sat behind the wheel. He left the motor running as he swung open the little door and jumped down and went over to Helmina, who stood watching. She hadn't cared to get too close.

"Well, Helmina, what do you think of it?"

Helmina looked at him.

"Martin, look at you! How did you ever get your nice suit so dusty?"

He looked down at his suit and brushed some dust off his knees.

"In the back, Martin!"

Helmina tried to brush the back of his suit jacket.

Martin was an immaculate dresser, and he was a little annoyed that his suit was dirtied. "I knew I should have bought one of those long washable coats that auto drivers wear!"

He proceeded to explain the cause. "I know how I got so dirty. There is that chain underneath the auto that makes the wheels turn, and it kept slipping off . . . so I had to lie down underneath the machine and get it back on. It happened three times on the way from Canton. But it is quite a machine, don't you think? I've come to give you a ride."

"Why don't you shut your car off and stay and eat with us? We can have rides after dinner."

Helmina was thinking that the confusion and noise would scare the horses when the teams came home.

Martin turned off the motor and then walked around his automobile, dusting off the fenders and brushing some more on his suit. Then he noticed it! One of the hind car lamps was missing! He wondered where it was. It must have fallen off some place between there and Canton. The dirt road today had some deep dried up ruts in several places, which made rough riding. He figured it had been shaken loose in one of those spots. He would have to check on the way back and see if he could find it.

When the men came with the teams and hayrack, they watered their horses, put them in the barn to eat and rest, and then headed for the new auto to inspect it.

"How about a ride, Martin?" Hans asked.

"Sure. I'll give you all a ride."

By now, Obed and Thelma and Bertha and Helmina and the men were all gathered around the machine.

"Have we time to go for a spin before dinner, Hemmy?"

"I guess dinner will wait," she replied.

"Come, Ole, you sit here by me, and Helmina and Obed and Thelma can sit in the back seat. You too, Bertha!"

Helmina hesitated. "Well now, Martin, are you sure it will be safe for the children to go?"

"Oh, I won't drive fast. We'll just go down to the corner and come slowly back. Then I'll give the rest a ride."

Ole climbed into the front seat and Helmina reluctantly stepped into the back seat.

Now Martin got out the crank and went to the front of the car and began cranking it to get it started. Several times it made a noise as if it was going to start, and then died. The third time he turned the crank, the motor took off, and the whole machine began to vibrate. Helmina put Thelma in her lap and held Obed's hand. She wished she had something to hang on to.

Martin climbed behind the wheel, put the car in gear, and the noisy machine began moving. Martin drove very slowly to the end of the lane, turned around and returned. When he got in the yard, he put on the brakes and when it came to a stop, the passengers got out.

Reinert, Hans, and Uncle Chris got in. Now the machine was warmed up, and so Martin stepped on the gas and gave the men a faster ride, even thirty miles an hour on the ride to the corner east and back.

Ole didn't care for the ride. He much preferred the smooth, quiet progress of a team and buggy.

Everyone came in to eat. During dinner Martin was telling about the enthusiastic Beresford auto drivers who these past months had been racing from Beresford to Canton in one hour and thirty minutes. They would travel in a procession, and when they arrived in Canton, they would turn down Fifth Street toward the Rudolph Hotel and toot their tooters and sit back with heads erect and smile, as if to say, "Look at us. We came to your autoless town on a canter of one hour and thirty minutes."

"The Canton buggy drivers and bike pushers had stood this thing long enough," Martin said, "so Canton's Superintendent of the electric light plant, W. P. Storie, bought a big Rambler. *And do you know what?* He took a trip to Beresford and as he gave a good-bye toot to Beresford, the Canton machine covered the 25 miles in one hour and 15 minutes, including stops and slow-ups for frightened teams."

Martin took another helping of potatoes and gravy, and finished off his meat, leaving everyone time to consider the Beresford-Canton auto rivalry.

"After finishing the clearance sale of the store several weeks ago," Martin went on, "I decided Canton should get into the auto competition and ordered this car. Four other Canton men are getting new cars this week also."

"What are you going to do now that your store is closed?" Nordlie asked.

"I'm going to Minneapolis next week! I'm going to check out a business proposition."

He looked at his sister. "Hemmy, how would you like to go along?"

She didn't know quite what to say.

"In your auto?" she asked, as she looked at Martin with a startled expression.

"No, I'm not ready for that! I'm going to take the train. I'll check out a new business there that is looking for salesmen for carbide lights.

"With everything getting modern now-a-days, with telephones and cars, I think the next thing people will want are lights in their homes. Kerosene and Aladdin lamps are nothing in comparison with these carbide lights. Everyone will want them.

"Yes, I'm going to take the train. Sister Anna has been there visiting for over a month, you know, and her friend, Anna Jacobson, plans to go along also. We'll all meet down there. *Why don't you come too?*"

Helmina glanced at Ole and then said, "Well, I could visit Aunt Helmine. I haven't seen her for many years."

Helmina Narum Opsahl, Johanna's sister, had married in 1889, and now lived north of Minneapolis.

"And I would like to do some shopping. I'll call you after we talk it over."

Martin got up and excused himself because he had to go and look for his auto lamp.

Helmina reminded him, *"Drive carefully, Martin. Don't go so fast."*

Martin turned around at the door and replied, "Don't worry. I'll let the others do the racing. I just want this machine to get me where I want to go. *And I have to be especially careful when I drive in Canton.*"

He had had his hand on the doorknob, but now he walked back to the table again, for he had some information to share. "Last Wednesday a big red auto came through Fifth Street in Canton *at 40 miles an hour.* A horse of J. A. Carpenter's, tied in front of the telephone office, became frightened and in a few jumps broke loose and ran away, leaving the buggy behind. It cost the driver $10 and costs.

"Six miles an hour is the speed limit in Canton, and four miles at intersections. I don't want to give the city my money so I'll be careful."

The men followed Martin outside and watched as he went through the process of cranking and getting the automobile in gear and then setting off down the road to Canton, leaving a trail of dust behind.

Chapter XXV

Helmina came with the broom and dust pan, and Bertha carried the dust rag in her hand as they entered the dining room. They had a job ahead of them — to clean up after the workmen who had been installing the new lights. Bits of plaster and dust had fallen when the workmen had attached the little pipes that carried the carbide to the light fixtures in the dining room and kitchen. A layer of dust was everywhere. These pipes were hooked up to a tank that stood in the back entry.

Martin had taken the salesman job from the carbide company when he was in Minneapolis in August. He had gotten his mother's permission to install the first carbide lights in the Overseth home, where Nordlies lived. When people could see how well these worked, he was sure more people would be ordering.

Helmina swept the debris into the dust pan and then got the dust mop and went over her wooden dining room floor. Bertha dusted all the chairs and the table. Together they moved the table back into the center of the room, right under the new fixture, and put the chairs in place. They then cleaned up the kitchen and got the supper on the table.

It was the last of November and the days were getting shorter. Darkness began to creep in about five o'clock. Helmina got the matches and reached above the table to light the new apparatus.

"Now, let me see," she said. "I must remember how I was to do this."

She turned the spigot and then put the lit match to it, and a flame began to burn. The room gradually turned from dusk to light.

When the men came in for supper, they were very impressed. They sat down around the table under the new light. Helmina took one look at *Obed and exclaimed, "Obed, you forgot to wash. Look at your hands! And Thelma, you too! Where have you been?"*

"We were just playing outside with Curl and Carlo," Thelma explained.

This year Obed was staying home and attending the Rise School. Each day he rode Bessy the mile and a half to and from school and was home soon after four o'clock.

Both the children got up from the table and went out to the wash basin. When Obed came back, he said as he sat down, "I don't know if I'm going to like these new lights. They *SEE* everything."

While the family was eating supper, the telephone rang. Nordlie got up and went to the kitchen to answer it.

"It was Maria Johnson from across the road. She wanted to know if the lights were in and if they could come and see them."

As Ole sat down he added, "They'll be over in a little while."

The family finished eating and Helmina and Bertha hurried to get the dishes done. Helmina had just spread her embroidered tablecloth on the dining room table when the Johnsons' buggy drove up.

Maria rushed into the house while August tied the horses.

Ole opened the door for Maria, and she was barely inside when she began exclaiming *"Oh SEE! Oh SEE! I never believed it would be this bright."*

She took off her coat and gave it to Ole, who was waiting for it. *"It is almost like daytime,"* she said.

"Yah," Nordlie agreed, "now I can read my paper every night by a good light."

Maria went closer to the light, and then she looked down at the large print apron she was wearing. *"Oh NEI! Oh NEI! I didn't know my apron was so dirty! Oh nei, oh nei!"*

She was more surprised than embarrassed.

"Oh, that's alright, Maria," Helmina assured her. "You are fine."

"It's funny, though," Maria explained, "because at home it looked like my apron was clean."

August came in and was impressed with the carbide lights also. After Ole showed them the pipes and the tank in the entry, Helmina had them sit down around the table, and she brought in coffee. The hired men decided to have 'another cup' too. She put the sugar lumps and cream on the table, and a plate of doughnuts. No one was very hungry as they had just finished supper.

Sitting around the table drinking coffee, they discussed the happenings in the community. The big news that week was that Adolph Gubbrud, the present proprietor of the Moe Store, was having a big *close-out sale* in December. And furthermore, their neighbor, Knute Rise, had decided to take over the store, which meant his farm on the west side of Overseth's would be for rent.

Hans Rognlien quickly spoke up. "I am trying to rent it."

Ever since Hans had come to Dakota, he had been on the look-out for a farm to rent.

"So, Nordlie," August pointed out, "then you will lose one of your hired men!"

"Yah, that is true, but he won't be far away and I hope we'll see a lot of him even if he becomes a farmer," Nordlie said.

August and Nordlie went over the changes at the Moe Store through the years.

"I remember how handy it was for us when Button and Olson first built the store," August said. "We didn't have to go way to Canton or Hudson for supplies."

"And then Oluf Ekle bought in as a partner to Button. I remember how Oluf and his violin would entertain the people gathered there in the evenings," Nordlie recalled.

August went on, "Yah, then Claus Hegness and Knute Jacobson took over, and there were many changes at Moe. They started selling John Deere farm machinery and built the town hall."

"NOW another Knute will be proprietor—Knute Rise."

"Yah, so it goes," August summed it up. "But Moe is more than a store. As long as they keep it open, it will be a meeting place, especially for the men of the community in the evenings."

Helmina passed the *sukkerbits* and the men each took one. Then they busied themselves dipping the little cubes into their coffee and quickly depositing them in their mouths.

"Say, Ole, did you read in the paper about the new law in Canton," August asked. *"No spitting on the sidewalks!"*

"Yah, there are going to be some tobacco-chewers that will have a time with that!"

Helmina interrupted. "I'm glad. There have been times when I've been shopping that I've had to lift my skirts so I wouldn't get them edged with tobacco juice. It was so unsanitary!"

"Yes," Ole added, "Now that they are laying nice sidewalks, it makes sense to keep them clean."

Helmina tried to pass the doughnuts again, but August and Maria decided it was time to go home.

As Maria put on her coat, she looked at her apron again and laughed. "I can't believe I left home with such a dirty apron."

Everyone joined in, and laughed with her.

"Yah, that's the way it is when you have carbide lights," Ole said.

He opened the door for them and they went out into the darkness for the buggy ride home.

Curl, the Nordlie's black dog, had been lying on the front porch for over an hour. Ever so often it would raise its head and perk up its ears as if it heard something, only to put its head down again. This time it perked up its ears, got to its feet and trotted off down the driveway.

It was a week before Christmas, 1906, and this morning Ole Nordlie had taken the lumber wagon filled with oats and headed for the Canton grain elevator. Today he was going to sell oats and do his Christmas shopping. Also, he had a long list of supplies to purchase for Helmina.

At the Anderson Furniture Store, Ole had found a beautiful oil painting which he thought Helmina would like. It would be especially nice in the parlor when they moved back to their own home again. He had purchased a locket for Thelma at the jewelry store and bought a wood-burning set for Obed to experiment with.

All day Ole had hurried with his errands, and was pleased to be on the road for home before four o'clock. Now he was almost home, but darkness was setting in. His spirits lifted as he saw a shadowy form approaching them. Good old faithful Curl had heard him coming and had come to meet him. The dog followed the wagon into the farm yard, wagging its tail all the way.

Ole tied the horses by the back gate and unloaded the groceries and supplies for Helmina. The long list had included oysters, lingonberries . . . and a Christmas tree, which he left outside by the back entry.

The hired men hadn't come in for supper yet, so he parked the wagon, unhitched the horses, and then carried his Christmas packages up into the hayloft of the barn for safe keeping until Christmas.

"*I got my Christmas shopping done today*," Ole announced at the supper table.

"Did you buy a present for me, Papa?" Thelma asked.

"You'll have to wait and find out a week from tonight," he replied.

"Pa," Obed pointed out, "I haven't had a chance to do my Christmas shopping yet."

"Well, Obed," his father suggested, "why don't you and Thelma drive over to Moe Store tomorrow and do your shopping? You'll be nine years old in a couple of days, so you are old enough to go by yourself. You can manage Bessy all right."

This made Obed feel very grown-up. It was Christmas vacation, so Bessy and he didn't have to go to school. The next day, right after the noon meal, Obed and Thelma put on their coats, caps and mittens and headed for the store. Knute Rise, the new proprietor, had already gotten in much new merchandise. Obed and Thelma took their time looking around, trying to get ideas for the gifts for their parents.

They discovered some new pieces of china with beautiful flowers painted on the cups and saucers. They decided to get a cup and saucer with roses on it for their mother.

It was more difficult finding something for their father.

"Pa is always happy with the suspenders we've bought him other years," Obed said. "That's something he always needs."

"I'll help you pick out a pair," Thelma offered.

They brought their purchases to Knute.

"You have made some good choices," the proprietor told them. "Let's see, you have a cup and saucer. Now all you need is some silverware."

He turned around and took something off his shelves. It was a can of baking powder, with a shiny silver spoon attached.

"See, you can get this spoon FREE if you buy this can of baking powder. Baking powder is something your mother always needs!"

"Let's get that too, Obed!" Thelma coaxed.

Obed thought that would be a good idea too, so they had the storekeeper wrap up their packages for they didn't want their parents to get a glimpse of their purchases. When they got home, Obed hid the gifts under his bed.

The next morning at breakfast, as everyone sat around the table, Ole Nordlie, with a twinkle in his eye, began to tell about the dream he had had during the night.

He took his time as he put the thin grape jelly on his cream and bread and took a few bites. Finally, he looked from one of his children to the other and said, *"I dreamed it was Christmas Eve and we were opening our packages, and do you know what I got?"*

He paused a moment, and then added, ". . . *a pair of suspenders!"*

"Papa, that's not fair! You aren't supposed to guess!" Thelma was upset with her father.

"But Mama, you can never guess what we bought YOU!" Thelma blurted out, "It's sour."

And Obed added,". . . and it shines like the sun!"

"It's sour and shines like the sun? That's a difficult thing to guess. All I can think of that's sour is sour milk . . . or vinegar!"

"No, that's not it!" Thelma quickly responded.

"I know!" their mother made another guess. "If it shines like the sun, it must be a mirror!"

"No, wrong again!" Thelma answered.

"I guess I'll have to take some time to think this over before I make any more guesses."

Helmina tried all week to figure out this puzzle, but she didn't come up with the right answer . . . and Obed and Thelma didn't give her any more hints. She really was surprised when she opened her gift and found a can of baking powder . . . and the beautiful shiny silver spoon! . . . and the cup and saucer.

Every day Ole was quick to get to the mailbox, and everyday he came into the house disappointed because he hadn't received any Christmas letters from Norway. To him, it didn't seem like Christmas until he got his mail from Norway.

On the second day of Christmas, church services were held at the Trinity Church and the Nordlie family attended. That day their neighbor down the road, Mrs. Christopherson, came with her bag full of Christmas postcards. Again, this year the mailman had been bringing all the postcards that people had written "*Merry Christmas*" on to the Christophersons. She spent time both before and after church delivering brightly colored Christmas postcards to many of the families on the Hudson mail route.

Mrs. Christopherson gave the Nordlies a number of cards too. Ole looked through them but none were from Norway. If they had been in Norwegian, the mailman probably would have had no trouble reading "*God Jul*" (Merry Christmas), but as a newcomer who hadn't lived many years in America, he thought when people wrote "*Merry Christmas*" they were trying to spell "*Christopherson.*"

Maria Johnson stopped Helmina in church and told her they should come to the Trinity Sunday School program that evening. "All of the girls have pieces to speak, and Hermand and three other boys will sing in a quartet. It'll be a fine program."

Helmina promised her family would come.

The Nordlies got to Trinity early that evening because with such favorable weather, the seats would fill up fast. They sat in the same row as August and Maria, right behind the Sunday School children.

After the Sunday School had sung several Christmas songs, it was time for Esther Johnson to give the welcome. She was twelve years old now and had on the new dress her sister Anna had sewn for her. Anna had sewn new dresses for all of her sisters.

As Esther walked up the two steps in the front of the church, her mother, Maria, leaned her large body forward, grasping the back of the pew in front of her. As Esther began to speak, Maria mouthed every word. But Esther needed no help, and Maria gave a deep breath and slumped back into her pew.

Later, when Ruth had a piece to speak, Maria again leaned forward, grasping the back of the pew ahead of her and silently mouthed Ruth's part. And later, when the little girls, Augusta and Judith, stood with the other younger children to recite their one line each, Maria again went through the same process.

Maria was a mother who was deeply involved with her children's lives and always tried her best to have them do well.

That evening, Obed and Thelma got more enjoyment out of watching Maria than listening to the Sunday School Christmas program.

Chapter XXVI

"The winter is long for those who tend livestock.*" Ole Nordlie had
Hannah Vinsness' *'Dairymaid'* poem running through his mind
today. He was busy cleaning in the cow barn. Finally, he took the pitch
fork and spread fresh straw in each stall. Yah, he thought, tonight the
cows will have a clean place to lie.

Outside the farmyards were a March mire. After the first week in
March, the temperature had risen, melting the snow and taking the frost
out of the ground. The animals walked around in knee-deep mud. Yah,
the winter may be tedious and long . . . but taking care of the livestock
in a muddy March can be worse. The animals had nowhere to lie down
but in the mud. At least, the milk cows would find something solid and
clean to lie on during the night.

But really, these first few months of 1907 hadn't been long. This
winter hadn't held the usual quiet days of a farm winter. There had been
too much happening.

In January, their neighbor, Knute Rise, had his farm sale, and when
the first of March had come, Nordlie's hired man, Hans Rognlien, had
left to farm the Rise place. On March 5th, Helmina's brother, Johnny,
had had an auction sale on his farm down by Hudson. He would be moving to Canton when the roads got in better shape.

Yes, things had really been happening. Johnny Overseth had rented
his Hudson farm to his two younger brothers, Jim and Henry, and they
and their mother Johanna would be moving out there. Johnny and his
family would live in Johanna's home in Canton while their new home
was being built.

Ole had a good feeling about this move. He felt that in a year or
two, after the boys had had some experience farming, they could take

over the Overseth farm; and then he and his family could move home . . ."*and then we can make that trip to Norway!*"

Tomorrow, the 30th, Helmina and he would have to go to Canton to make the final arrangements for purchasing the eighty acres from Hillarius Tollefsrud. He dreaded the trip, with the roads in such bad shape.

Ole turned around as he heard someone open the barn door. He supposed it was Reinert, who had been feeding the cattle, but he was surprised and pleased to see his old hired man, Hans Rognlien.

"Hello, Hans! You looking for work?"

"No, I have plenty to do at the Rise place. I just picked up the mail, and I got a letter from my mother. *Have you heard from Norway lately?*"

"No. I didn't even get my Christmas letters. I don't know what is wrong over there. I guess they have forgotten about me."

Ole leaned on his pitch fork. "Well, is there any news from Hurdal?"

Hans took the letter out of his pocket and began to open it. "*Yes, but it isn't good news.*"

"Is someone sick?" Ole asked.

Hans fidgeted with the pages and finally he said, "Let me read it to you."

He began to read what his mother had written about their family, and then he went on . . .

"My neighbor was over yesterday, and he had the saddest news. I suppose Ole Christian has already heard about it. Marte Nordlien died last week, February 27th. He said the funeral would be March 15th. I suppose Otto and Ingeborg will be coming over from Toten . . ."

As Hans read on, Ole didn't hear the rest of the letter. The words "*Marte Nordlien died*" had stuck in his heart like a knife blade. Was he really hearing this? *Mother dead? No, it couldn't be!* . . . now that he was so close to his Norway trip.

Ole interrupted Hans' reading with "*No! No! No!*" half weeping and half pleading. "*Tell me it isn't true.*"

Ole covered his face with his mittened hands and tried to hold back the sobs.

"I'm sorry, Ole. I'm so sorry," Hans comforted, but Ole turned away and climbed upstairs into the hayloft. Here he lay face down in the hay and sobbed.

I thought I was so close to seeing her again. But now it shall never be. But even worse than that, I didn't keep my promise to return.

All Ole could see in his mind's eye was his mother's farewell when he left Norway as she stood there wiping her eyes with her apron. He could still hear himself promise, *"I'll be back again, Mother. I promise."*

Finally he just let the sobs loose, for he realized that now it was too late. His dear little mother was gone.

Hans went into the house and told Helmina the sad news. "This will be hard on Ole," she told him.

"Yes, I'm afraid so," Hans agreed.

Helmina poured up some coffee and invited Hans to sit down. After awhile Ole came into the house, but he had no desire for food. He sat down by the dining room table and began to ask Hans questions.

"When did you say she died?"

"February 27th"

"And what was the date of the funeral?"

"The 15th."

"That was two weeks ago! And I wasn't there!" Ole realized that the rest of the family most likely had gathered to lay her to rest . . . *but he had been missing for that too!*

Hans got to his feet to leave, "I imagine you'll be getting a letter soon from Ingeborg and Otto, and then you can get the details."

After Hans left, Helmina put her arm around her husband and repeated, *"I'm so sorry. I'm so sorry."* But he turned his head away from her. He didn't want to start sobbing again.

"Are you sure you can't drink some coffee and have a sugar lump?" Helmina coaxed. She knew that he usually found comfort in coffee and sugar lumps.

Ole mumbled "no," lay his head on his arm, and he just sat there at the dining room table. Helmina went into the kitchen.

Soon Obed and Thelma came home from Norwegian Parochial School. This school had begun as soon as the six-month regular school term was over.

Helmina whispered, "Sh-hhhh. Don't go in the dining room. Papa has had some bad news. *Gramdma Marte died,* and Papa feels so bad. Here, sit down and have a cookie and some milk."

But Obed and Thelma were curious and both went to the door and peeked. They saw their father with his head cradled in his arm. They then realized the seriousness of this news. Papa was always on top of his problems and difficulties, and now they saw things could hurt him too.

Several weeks later, Ole received a letter from his sister Ingeborg and her husband Otto.

Dear Ole,

We have some very sad news to give you. Mother is gone. She passed away on February 27th after several months of not feeling well. She had been having bad head aches and she died from a severe stroke.

The funeral was March 15th. We went down in the sleigh the day before and took along meat from a sheep we butchered, and also bread and *totenkringler* Ingeborg had baked, to be used for the meal after the funeral.

Your mother had many relatives in the community and the church was almost full, which was unusual for this time of the year. The pastor had a fine message, using the text from Revelation 14:13.

Ole got out the big Bible and looked up the verse. *"Blessed are the dead who die in the Lord . . ."*

He thought about the words. *". . . die IN THE LORD"*

Yes, Ole had seen his mother on her knees by her bed in prayer. She knew the Lord.

"Yea, that they may rest from their labors." Yes, now Mother could rest from her hard and busy life. Rest. At peace. With the Lord.

Ole was so glad they had included the text. Now he felt like he had a little part in her funeral.

Ole went back to the letter again.

We know this will be a shock to you and we know you will be grieving also, even as we are here. As a son-in-law, I can only say, "You had a fine mother."

We'll write more later.

Your brother-in-law,
Otto Rognlien

The farming year of 1907 was a busy one for Ole Nordlie. With the two extra Tollefsrud eighties to be farmed, and minus one hired man, Ole himself put in long, laborous days. But it felt good to be busy.

With Helmina's mother at the Hudson farm, Helmina this year did most of her shopping in Hudson, which was a lesser distance than to Canton. On the way home, she would always stop to see her mother.

"*Nei,* Helmina," her mother always insisted, "you and the children must stay and have supper with us." Today she coaxed them as usual.

"Well, I am a little late, and I don't want to be on the road after dark," Helmina explained.

"We're ready to eat now, before the boys do the chores."

Helmina always used the one horse buggy, with Bessy, but on every trip she had this deep fear of being met on the road by an automobile.

Johanna passed the bread and cheese and the warmed over potatoes.

As they ate, Helmina was brought up-to-date on the members of the family.

"Mother, have you heard from Martin and Tony lately?" Helmina asked.

"I received a card a couple of days ago," she replied. "They'll be home the end of next week."

This past year Tony had attended business college at Grand Island, Nebraska, and in May when the session was over, Martin met him down there and the two of them went on to St. Louis, where they joined the band that played with a big carnival. They had spent the summer traveling to the west coast and back.

"What do you hear from Anna then?"

"She's planning to stay in Minneapolis and take some courses at an art school there this fall. I think it has something to do with her friend working near there. He has finished St. Olaf College now and is teaching near there.

"Yah, Hans Dale and Anna have been close friends ever since Augustana days. They'd never get to see each other if she was here in South Dakota."

When everyone was through eating, Helmina hurried the children out to the buggy so they could start home. Uncle Christian, who was staying with Johanna and the boys now, went out to untie the horse for Helmina.

When they had gotten two miles down the road, Helmina thought she heard something, and as she got farther west, it got louder. Then she saw a trail of dust rising up ahead. Helmina was almost to a road intersection so she turned Bessy north at the crossing and they sat and waited until the noisy monster had gone by. Bessy was not as nervous as some of the horses, who rose up on their hind legs, and took for the ditches which were usually filled with water, when an auto approached them.

Helmina was glad to get home again. The roads were no longer the safe places they used to be before the invention of the automobile.

Chapter XXVII

Helmina sat at the dining room table, a big length of white linen cloth spread out before her. She was working along one side of the material, using a new stitch—pulling out some threads and weaving remaining ones. This open strip of fancywork would be worked on all four sides and would make this white linen material into an elegant tablecloth.

She sat at the dining room table under the carbide lights so she could work at night. Ole sat at the other end of the table reading the Canton newspaper.

"Ole," Helmina interrupted his reading, "do you think you and Reinert can take the carpets out one of the next days and beat them? The April weather is nice now and I should get busy with spring housecleaning if we are going to have a wedding here in several months."

Ole looked up from his paper. "We perhaps can take time to do it in the morning. The oats are all in the ground and the other jobs around the place can wait a day."

Helmina worked for a while on her sewing project. She glanced at Ole from time to time, and finally she spoke.

"Also, Ole," she said, "there is something else I've been wanting to talk to you about."

She laid down her sewing and studied him carefully as she approached the subject.

"I don't know how you'll feel about this."

She slipped off her thimble and placed it on the table, then raised her head to look at him.

". . . I wonder if we could get a piano before the wedding."

Ole dropped his paper and sat erect.

"What do you need a piano for when you have an organ? That should be good enough."

"No, Ole," she explained, "you don't understand. Anna would like to have a piano so Miss Dokken can play the wedding march, and Martin wants a piano to accompany the musical group that will play that day. He says it isn't the same with an organ."

She paused for a moment and then added, "And besides, when we move home we can take the piano along and Thelma can take music lessons. Pa's old organ will stay here."

The idea of Thelma taking piano lessons interested Ole.

"Do you know how much it would cost?" he asked.

"No, but we have time to check around."

Anna Overseth and Hans M. Dale had set the date of their wedding for June 30, 1908. Anna wanted to have the ceremony in the Overseth homestead instead of at the church. They were going to get a kneeler built that they could use in the parlor for the wedding.

Anna wanted to get married in the home she had grown up in, and it would only be a family affair.

Helmina was making the new tablecloth to be used that day. All the table leaves would need to be inserted to accommodate the wedding party and guests, and that required a large tablecloth.

Helmina also had to begin sewing the white organdy and eyelet dress for Thelma because she would be one of the flower girls.

The two months passed quickly, and Helmina and Bertha were busy with cleaning and preparations. The last two weeks before the wedding, Anna came from Minneapolis to help with the plans. Many flowers were blooming that they could use in the vases on the table and in the baskets in the parlor.

On Tuesday, June 30th, the weather was pleasant. Soon after noon the groom's relatives arrived from Howard, South Dakota. His sister, and a good friend of Anna's would be her attendants, and his niece would be the other flower girl. Anna's brother, James, would be best man.

At three o'clock the bride and her attendants were all assembled upstairs, and the groom and his best man stood at the foot of the open staircase in the dining room. The guests were all seated, the members of the musical ensemble were in place, and Pastor Nummedal waited by the padded kneeler in the parlor. Several large baskets of flowers stood around him.

When Miss Dokken played the first strains of the wedding march, the bridesmaids began their descent, followed by Nellie Buck and Thelma, the two flower girls. They carried baskets filled with roses and sweet peas. Ever so often they would pull out a blossom and drop it.

Lastly, came the bride in her beautiful white gown. She carried a bouquet of pink roses. At the bottom of the staircase the best man and groom met the bride and attendants, and the procession proceeded through the dining room into the parlor.

The flower girls spread their blossoms along the way. When Thelma walked past Anton Stikbakke, the clarinetist, he picked up the flower and gave it back to her, whispering, "You dropped something." Thelma gave him a piercing look and continued on her way to the flowery bower in the parlor where Pastor Nummedal waited.

Thelma and Obed enjoyed all the excitement of the wedding preparations. A new piano was sitting in the dining room. This was exciting. And this morning they had sneaked down into the cellar where all kinds of delicious foods were kept. They had had their first taste of fresh pineapple, which would be used in the salad. They had gotten to sample the ice cream as they sat alongside their father as he cranked out two large batches of homemade ice cream. And this was the first time they had experienced dinner music. While the guests ate, and during the evening, Martin's little orchestra played.

Helmina had been very busy, but she enjoyed providing a lovely wedding for her sister. However, Ole was getting tired of all the fussing and was looking forward to life getting back to normal again. He had bought the piano . . . but it was for Thelma so she could take piano lessons.

The week after the wedding as Ole was reading the weekly *Dakota Farmers Leader*, he came across the item about the wedding.

Dale - Overseth Wedding

One of the most delightful home weddings ever witnessed in Norway Township took place at the home of Mrs. O. Overseth at 3 o'clock Tuesday afternoon, June 30, in the presence of relatives and a few close friends assembled to witness the marriage of Hans M. Dale and Miss Anna Overseth and the ceremony performed by Rev. Nummedal of Lands. The bride was attended by Nellie Dale of Northfield, sister of the groom, and Bertha Salveson of Sioux Falls, while the groom's best man was James Overseth. Flower girls were Nellie Buck and Thelma Nordlie.

A piano and orchestra furnished music, the piano being presided over by Miss Dokken and Miss Salveson and the orchestra composed by Martin and Anton Overseth, Anton Bakke and Gust Dokken and his brother.

A grand wedding dinner followed at the home of Mrs. Overseth and the wedding festivities continued until a late hour.

The bride is a daughter of the late Ole Overseth of Norway Township and was born in the home where the ceremony took place. She is a charming young lady and has won an accomplished gentleman as life partner. Professor H. M. Dale is a member of the Augustana faculty.

Ole read the newspaper report again. He took a deep breath and then uttered a loud *"Hmmmph."* He laid the paper down, puzzled as to who had given that wedding report to the editor.

After the wedding, Helmina lost her good house helper. Bertha Blom was young, and she wanted to get a job in town. When Ole and Helmina heard the Rev. Tetlies in Canton were looking for help, Bertha and Helmina had contacted them. After the wedding Bertha went to work in the Lutheran parsonage in Canton.

Helmina really missed Bertha. She was always going around dusting and cleaning. Helmina had depended so much on her.

Obed and Thelma spent a delightful summer. There were fish in the creek, and Obed often sat down on the bridge and went fishing. Their daily companions were their dogs, Carlo and Curl.

That spring Helmina put some goose eggs under several of her setting hens and soon six little geese began waddling around the barnyard. They were cute until they grew older and decided to nest by the water tank, where they were vicious to anyone who came near.

Ole put in long days that summer and often was very tired. He still had Reinert but he really missed Hans, especially at haying time. But though he was busy here with his South Dakota farming, his thoughts frequently returned to his old home *Nordlien,* sitting high up on the side of Nordli Kampen.

In October he sat down and wrote to his sister and brother-in-law.

Dear Brother-in-law, Otto,

I received your letter a while ago. I had begun to believe you had decided to stop your correspondence with me, so when your letter arrived it was much welcome, and dear to me. So I want to give you my heartiest thanks.

It pleases me to hear that everything is well with you there at home, and I can tell the same from here. We are now busy picking corn, which this year seems to be a large crop, and the price is very good so the farmers here are doing well this year, both with crops and income. The price on other grains is also high, so if you there in Norway are importing wheat and corn from here it will cost you more. But I don't plan to sell my corn, but will turn it into beef and pork. I am feeding 40 steers, 3 years old, and am fattening them, feeding them all they will eat, and will sell them about the 1st of April so it will take about 4000 bushel for that. Then I have 75 hogs besides. When I have sold them all, I will write and tell you what my profits were. I now have, counting young and fullgrown cattle, 100 head, also have 13 horses, 75 hogs and my son Obed has 7 sheep, so there are many to feed my grain to. It is raining here now so we are delayed with the corn picking. The grass is still green yet.

Now you can believe we are deep in politics here. We have President election in two weeks, and the campaign is more violent than we have ever seen it. But it isn't only the President we will elect, but also the state officers, all along the line. The candidates for President, Republican is William H. Taft, and the Democrat is William Brian (Bryan). The Democrats are working hard to regain the power in Congress, which they haven't had since the time of Cleveland. Their candidate is running the third time and we hope he loses again. People still remember the low prices and hard times we had when they steered the government. Well, I guess this is all about politics.

I feel bad about Mathilda, that things aren't good. It is sad that she has no home of her own. It seems her husband should get a place so they shouldn't be living so poor. I must close for now. Greet all my relatives in Toten, and if possible in Hurdalen. You and your family are all greeted from me and mine.

Ole Nordlie

"You'd better have a second helping, Hans," Helmina said as she passed the roast beef, potatoes and gravy again. "*Vaer saa god.* Help yourself."

Every week Hans Rognlien came home from church with the Nordlies and ate Sunday dinner with them. Ole looked forward to this, and in the afternoon the two would visit. This week in November, Hans had received a letter from his mother so he had the latest Hurdal news to share.

Usually on Sunday afternoons some of Helmina's family stopped in. Today it was Jim and Henry and Helmina's mother, Johanna. Later, Martin and Tony drove up in Martin's new car. The brothers were now living in Fairview, South Dakota, a town half-way between Canton and Hudson, on the Iowa border. Here they had a hardware store, and here Professor Andrew Indseth, *the music man*, and his family now lived, and here he was organizing another band.

Soon Martin was at the piano playing and singing "*In My Merry Oldsmobile.*" He had sold his first auto to Segrud, the photographer in Canton, and now he was the owner of a new Oldsmobile. Soon others in the room gathered around him and they all began singing "*Barney Google*" and other fun ditties.

When Ole got up to go outside to check on his livestock, Jim arose too, made a comment that he wanted to see how Ole's cattle were doing, and followed him outside.

The two men stood leaning on the wooden fence and looking over the feeder cattle. Jim pointed out several animals that he felt were blue ribbon quality. His education at Agriculture College had given him an eye for quality.

"I think they'll be ready to sell in the spring," Ole said. "Maybe in March." They then discussed the cattle prices, and Jim told of the calves he had just purchased and the reasonable price he had paid.

Ole then climbed over the fence and went to the hay feeder where he took a pitch fork and moved hay closer to the openings so the cattle could reach it. He checked on the water supply in the tank and as the two of them walked through the barn, Jim stopped and admired the two new horses Ole had purchased.

Ole and Jim returned to the house where Helmina had the table laden with her Saturday baking and other good food. She was always prepared for Sunday company.

Today the table was full, and as everyone gathered around it to eat, there was a lot of joking and laughing. *But Ole had his thoughts on something else.*

After his visit outside with Jim, something had clicked. Ole now felt that Jim was ready for Overseth. It was time for the Nordlies to move home. *And he was glad.*

The Ole Nordlie family on their porch. Helmina, standing; Obed and father, Ole, seated; Thelma, with arm around her father; the dog, Curl, looking on.

Chapter XXVIII

Nordlie sat at the kitchen table in the early dawn. Today was March 20th, 1909. After starting a good fire in the cookstove and making coffee, he was sitting alone, going over all the events of the past month. He poured himself a cup of the hot liquid.

Yesterday he had returned from Chicago where he had shipped his fat cattle and hogs. It was almost amazing to him how well things had been working out. The prices had been good. The animals had been finished at the right time to sell before the move back to his farm, where there would not have been accommodations for all these animals if they had needed to be fed longer.

In two weeks his family would be moving back to their own farm, and today, with the big checks he had received in Chicago, he was considering some of the dreams he had laid aside.

A barn.. Yes, a large barn with room for horses, colts, cows, calves and lots of hay.

Ole poured himself some more hot coffee and sipped from his saucer.

And then there was the other dream . . . *the trip to Norway with his family*. Ole hardly dared to think of it because he knew it would be hard to go back now that his mother was gone. But he had promised his mother to return, and deep down inside he felt he had to go.

He took a sugar lump and dipped it in his cup, then placed the dripping sweet treat into his mouth. A strong longing to return welled up in him. He took a drink of coffee and then set the cup down.

Yes, they would go! He would talk it over with Helmina when she came down. He took another swallow of coffee and decided there was something about coffee and sugar lumps that helped him when he had to make decisions.

Ole had almost emptied his cup when Helmina joined him. He shared with her his ideas and plans, and right away she became excited about the trip . . . although she was a little surprised. She had not heard anything about the trip since his mother had died. But she was in full agreement.

"The children will love it," she assured him.

They sat and worked out the details. Reinert Linde, their hired man, had become like one of the family, and Ole wasn't worried about leaving him in charge of the farm. They would get a couple to help him — the woman could cook and keep house and her husband would help Reinert with the farm work.

Helmina poured some more coffee in Ole's cup when she filled her own. Yes, it would all work out well. Now they must get ready for the big move back to their own farm.

The first of May, after being settled on their own farm for five weeks, the Nordlie family began their trip to Norway. They boarded a ship in Montreal, Canada.

The first day took them up the St. Lawrence River. The next morning, Pentecost Sunday, the Nordlie family awoke and made plans to attend church services on board ship. Helmina put on the new black taffeta dress she had had the dressmaker sew for her.

But suddenly she felt sick . . . very sick. *Seasick*! She took to the bed and was not even able to get out of her nice dress.

Ole came into the room and saw her lying there, and asked, "What's the matter with you? You lay in bed with your best dress on?"

But in a short while he wasn't in any better shape. The ship had reached the Atlantic, and the majority of people on board had become seasick. However, Obed and Thelma hadn't. For the next two days, it was only an old sea captain and they who showed up for meals at their table for twelve in the dining room.

When the ship was about half way across the Atlantic, some of the ship's personnel went around making plans for a talent night. They approached Helmina and Ole, and at first they said they would not participate. When the man asked if their children couldn't do something, Helmina supposed Thelma could sing. She knew Thelma had learned many fun songs in school.

The night of the program Helmina dressed her eight-year-old daughter in the beautiful light blue wool dress she had sewn for her — the one with the wide fluted collar she had made with the fluting iron — and fixed her hair with a big bow.

Thelma happened to be the only child on the program. The Captain lifted her up on the stage and she sang the song she had learned in school, using the actions that went with it.

"I throw a kiss to daddy
    when he gets off the car.
Way up high he holds me
    and calls me his twinkling star.
There may be dads as nice as him
But I don't think there are
And then I kiss him lots of times
    when he gets off the car.

When she finished the song, she threw a kiss to the audience, and they clapped and clapped and clapped. Afterwards an English lady sent a box of candy to Thelma's room.

The ship landed in England and here the Nordlie family boarded another ship for Sweden. When they crossed the North Sea, it was Obed and Thelma's turn to get seasick.

A train took the family from Sweden, across the Swedish-Norwegian border, and into Christiania, the capital of Norway, where they spent one day shopping. Both Obed and Thelma got new coats. Thelma's had a large sailor collar, and she got the hat to go with it.

Helmina purchased a beautiful big black straw hat for herself at Steen and Strom. It was tastefully decorated with lovely flowers and was very fashionable.

Ole loaded the big trunk and their suitcases onto the train that would be stopping at Skreia, Eastern Toten, where both Ole's younger brother, Ludvig, and his sister, Ingeborg Rognlien, and her family lived. At these two homes, they spent the first few weeks in Norway.

The first morning at Rognlien's, as they were still lying in bed, there was a knock at their door and in marched Ingeborg with a tray of totenkringler and other rolls and cookies. Behind her was Otto with a tray of coffee cups and a coffee pot. Ole wasn't comfortable eating breakfast in bed, and he told them he would be downstairs for his coffee. But the children enjoyed all the good baking in the bedroom.

Now it was time to go home to Hurdal. Ole's brother, Ludvig, loaded up the trunk and suitcases in a wagon, and the family rode in a carriage across the Totenaasen to Hurdal.

Ole was anxious to go there, but also, he went with trepidation, knowing the old home wouldn't be the same because Mother wouldn't be there.

But they received a hearty welcome from his brother, Laurits, and wife, Karine, who made them feel at home.

Some things at Nordlien were changed, but the scenery was still the same — the mountains covered with evergreens and birch, the Nordlien forests, and the shining Hurdal Lake!

The second day he was there, Ole headed down the trail to the Hurdal church. On the way he picked some lily of the valley that were growing along the path. And when he got to the Hurdal church and the cemetery that surrounded it, he found his mother's grave. Seeing her grave finally made her death real to him. He stood there by himself for a long time. Finally he whispered, *"I came back, Mor. I'm sorry it wasn't sooner, but I did come back."* He laid the flowers on her grave and headed back up the mountain trail.

Ole was up early every day and was there to help his brother with the haying and other tasks, but Ole thought they spent too much time lunching. There was *"before breakfast lunch," "breakfast," "forenoon lunch," "middags," "afternoon lunch"* and *"supper."* They were always stopping to eat.

Ole had brought along denim bib overalls as gifts for his brothers and brothers-in-law. This was what men wore in America now.

"Aren't you going to wear your overall today?" Ole would ask his brother, but Laurits always answered, "No, not today."

Old dark wool trousers and shirts were the regular Norwegian work clothes.

The children enjoyed Karine. She was usually standing by the open fireplace in the kitchen and stirring in the big pot. When Obed and Thelma came in, they always asked her what she was making and she liked to tease them by saying, "Oh, I'm making pie!" Pie was not a familiar Norwegian food.

Often Laurits would send Obed and Thelma down to the valley to buy tobacco for his pipe. He would include a little extra money for candy.

The second week the Nordlie family was at Nordlien, Ole, in visiting with his brother, asked about the lumbering work.

"Which sections of the forest are you *felling* this year, Laurits?"

Finally, after some awkward moments, Laurits announced to Ole, "I am not doing lumbering any more. I sold the forests to Mathieson from the glass factory."

Ole couldn't believe what he was hearing. *"Sold the Nordlien forests? When did you do that?"*

"It's been hard times here, Ole, and after Mother died I sold them . . . and I may as well tell you the whole story. I sold *all* of Nordlien. I'm just renting the fields and buildings."

Ole became angry. "*Why didn't you let me know? Were you trying to keep it a secret?* You should have given me a chance to buy it. I'm the *second-born*."

"There's nothing we can do about it now," Laurits said, and walked away.

Ole didn't know what to do. He wanted to cry, but then he felt so angry that he wanted to shake his brother. Ole tried to remember that he was a guest here now, but he had to talk to someone. He went to the house and asked Helmina to go for a walk with him. The children followed along.

Helmina didn't know what was wrong. She could see that Ole was upset. As soon as they were away from the house, Ole blurted it all out. "*Laurits sold Nordlien that has been in our family for years. Can you believe it? HE SOLD IT!*" Then he put his hand over his face and tried to hold back the sobs.

". . . *And he didn't even give me a chance to buy it.* According to the *odelsret*, I should have had *first* chance. I'm the second-born." Ole choked back a sob again.

"And we had the money to buy it too! Instead of buying the Tollefsrud land, we could have bought *Nordlien. I can't believe it! I can't believe it!*"

Helmina tried to calm down her husband. The children had run ahead where they had found a wild strawberry patch.

"*Ole, I'm so sorry.* It is a shame! I know it is a terrible disappointment to you." Then she gave him a pleading look as she reminded him that they were guests there. "We have to act civil." Maybe you can go and talk to this Mathieson," she added.

Finally, Ole regained his composure, and after a long walk down to the creek and back up the trail again, they came to *Nordlien.* But Ole had a sharp pain in his heart, almost as bad as when he heard his Mother had died.

That afternoon he went by himself down the trail to the Hurdal church. He stood there by his mother's grave, and tried to sort things out. It was good his brother hadn't sold it while his mother was living. That would have hurt her terribly.

Ole then sat down on the church steps. At times flashes of anger welled up in him, and he thought he could never forgive his brother for what he had done. The worst thing about it was that Laurits hadn't given

him a chance to buy it. He was the second-born and that was his right.
He had had the money and he could have kept the *gaard* in the family.

But as he sat there thinking things through, it seemed he could hear
his mother's voice again, as she spoke twenty years ago, *"Oh, my boys!
Why can't you two get along? Will you be like Jacob and Esau, always
quarreling over each other's rights?"*

"Oh, Mother, it hurts so much. He overlooked my rights."

Ole knew this anger would only hurt himself, and make him unhappy, ruining the trip for the whole family. Yet by himself he knew he
couldn't conquer it.

He got up and walked around the church building. In the back of
the church he could see the mountains. As he was studying them, these
words from Psalms came to him.

*"I will lift up mine eyes unto the mountains,
from whence cometh my help."*

Ole turned his face upward and cried, *"Oh God, please help me. Take
away this awful anger in my heart."*

After a while, Ole headed back to *Nordlien*, which by right wasn't
Nordlien anymore, to face his brother, determined that he would not show
his anger and disappointment.

As he climbed the trail, he tried to find reasons for his brother's actions. Perhaps Laurits didn't have any other choice. Perhaps times had
really been difficult for him.

BUT it always came back to . . ."he should have let me know and
given me a chance!"

May, June, July and August quickly passed. The family visited other
relatives in Hurdal and Helmina's relatives in Vestre Toten. And when
Ole and Helmina sailed from Bergen to Trondheim, Obed and Thelma
visited at Stikbakkes.

Lastly, before the trip home, they came back to *Nordlien*. Brother
Laurits announced that he wanted to go along to Christiania with them
when they left, and bid them farewell. On the return trip, they would
sail from Norway instead of Sweden.

All in all, it had been a good trip, except for the news of the sale
of *Nordlien*. Everyone had been so gracious to them, especially Laurits
and Karine. Helmina, Obed and Thelma had enjoyed the beauty of Norway, and had gotten a chance to meet all of their relatives there.

At the harbor, as they loaded their trunk and suitcases on the ship, Ole glanced at his brother, Laurits, and the thought flashed through his mind that perhaps this would be the last time they would see each other. *Farewells could be so final.*

Finally, Ole and Helmina shook hands with Laurits for the last time, and heartily thanked him for his fine hospitality.

Ole stood by the rail as the ship slipped away from the dock. He could see his brother, Laurits, standing there, waving to them. There was something about the look on his face. Then it dawned on Ole how it must have pained Laurits to have to sell Nordlien, and how difficult it must have been for Laurits to tell him about it.

Obed and Thelma soon came to stand alongside their father. The dock was getting farther and farther away.

"Pa, aren't you glad we're going home?" Obed asked.

Going *home.*

Ole honestly could answer "Yes."

"Pa, do you think Carlo and Curl will remember me when we get home?" Thelma questioned.

Ole nodded his head and answered, "Sure, they will."

The children were soon on their way again to investigate the new ship. As Ole stood there, many thoughts were going through his mind.

Going home.

Yes, I think I've finally sifted through my feelings. Home is not here any more. Home is where my fields are, and our house is, . . . and where I am going to build a big fine barn.

The thought of the big barn excited him.

Yes, Reinert and I will be busy this fall. We must haul rocks and sand so I can get the barn up in the spring.

Now the land was far away. Ole put up his hand in a final wave.

Ole turned from the railing.

It must be almost coffee time. I think I'll find Helmina and go for a cup of coffee.

Maybe they'll have sugar lumps too!

Epilogue

In the summer of 1910, the year after the Norway visit, Ole Nordlie built a fine big barn on his farm in Norway Township in South Dakota. In 1919, he also built a beautiful spacious house. Ole kept farming on this land until the summer of 1935, when during the days of drought and the Depression, he suffered several heart attacks, and died in September of that year, at the age of 70.

In the 1920's, Ole and Helmina's two children were married: Obed, to a schoolteacher, Mabel Iverson; and Thelma, to a newcomer clerk at the Moe Store, Erling Fladmark. Ole and Helmina had seven grand-children: Obed's two daughter's, Eloise and Carol; and Thelma's five children, Doris, Kenneth,, Donald, Richard and Robert.

Following Ole's death, Obed and his family moved to the Nordlie farm, just west of the Lands church, where he farmed for a number of years. Several years before his death in 1983, Obed sold the building site to a great grandson of Ole and Helmina, James Stensland, who now lives with his wife, Patsy, and four children in the house that Grandpa built, where they look out upon the large barn he erected in 1910. Obed's daughters own the farm land.

After Ole's death, Helmina lived in Canton, Moe, and spent her final years in Sioux Falls, South Dakota, where she died in 1962, at the age of 86.

The hired man, Reinert Linde, worked for the Nordlies for another year, and then he was taken ill while visiting his cousin, Dr. L. J. Hauge, and died. He is buried on the Nordlie grave lot at Lands cemetery. The other hired man, Hans Rognlien, returned to Norway in 1914.

Professor Andrew Indseth, *the music man*, continued directing choirs and bands, and teaching vocal and instrumental music until February of 1912. He was stricken one evening after rehearsal of his band in Canton, and after suffering four days from a severe case of pneumonia, he passed away. He was a man rich in his love for music. At his funeral, the Fairview band played an appropriate band march, and *"Nearer My God To Thee."*

Back in Hurdal, Norway, Ole Nordlie's brother, Laurits, died in December of 1914. His son, Ole, took over *"Nordlien"* and was able to buy back the buildings and farm land. However, Mathieson would not sell the *Nordlien forests*. Next, Laurits' grandson, Ludvig, farmed *Nordlien* for a number of years until he passed away in 1982. Recently, the farm was purchased by a great granddaughter of Laurits, Inger Edel (Garsjø) Kopperud. Inger Edel and her husband, Leif, have beautifully restored the large house, and fixed the other buildings, so *Nordlien* is in the family today.

Several descendants of the *American*, Ole Nordlie, have visited *Nordlien* and have become acquainted with other *Nordlien* family members in Norway.